Welcome Home, Jellybean

Welcome Home, Jellybean

Marlene Fanta Shyer

Aladdin Paperbacks

Aladdin Paperbacks
An imprint of Simon & Schuster
Children's Publishing Division
1230 Avenue of the Americas
New York, NY 10020
Copyright © 1978 by Marlene Fanta Shyer
All rights reserved including the right of reproduction
in whole or in part in any form.
First Aladdin Paperbacks edition, 1988
Printed in the United States of America

Library of Congress Cataloging-in-Publication Data

Shyer, Marlene Fanta.
Welcome home, Jellybean.

SUMMARY: Neil's life turns upside down when his
parents take his retarded sister out of an institution and
bring her home to stay.
[1. Mentally handicapped—Fiction.   2. Brothers and
sisters—Fiction]   I. Title.
PZ7.S562We   1988   [Fic]   87-19483
ISBN 0-689-71213-8

15   17   19   20   18   16   14

*With thanks to
Joseph Colombatto, Director
of Woodhaven Center,
Temple University, who
thinks he knows all the
answers, and did.*

one

WHEN MY SISTER TURNED THIRTEEN THE SCHOOL
where she lived got her toilet-trained and my
mother decided she ought to come home to live,
once and for all.

My father and I weren't so sure, but he agreed
that we would all give it a try, and he and I got the
suitcase out of the storage room and loaded up the
trunk of the car and drove to the gas station to
have the tank filled while my mother was still up
in the apartment writing with the whipped-cream
squirter on a cake she had baked: WELCOME
HOME.

Which my sister of course cannot read.

My mother's idea was that my sister would be
able to taste WELCOME HOME and also appreciate a little bunch of flowers she put on the window
sill in her room, which used to be the dining room
until the superintendent, Mr. Parrish, had a wall

with a door in it put up and turned it into a bed-room.

I'm not sure what my father thought because he has just grown a new moustache, and his mouth disappears under it and it's hard to tell what his expression is. Usually when he drives he hums along with the car radio or complains about traffic, but it was my mother who seemed to be doing most of the talking today.

A few times she asked my father to slow down and then, when we passed a bunch of cows in a meadow, she said that my sister had probably never seen a cow in her life, or a horse.

Then she talked about a farm she'd visited one summer and she went on and on talking about how she had loved the chickens and pigs and used to shuck corn, which had nothing to do with anything. My father asked my mother why she was so nervous, and my mother said she wasn't nervous a bit, and she told my father to please slow down. To me she said, "Neil, please close the window," and a few miles later, when we'd stopped to eat our sandwiches, she turned right around and looked at me and said, "Why did you close your window, Neil?"

It seemed a longer drive than usual, but finally I could see the school in a valley below us, a whole bunch of green roofs a little darker than the houses in a Monopoly set, short roads between them and a few benches set here and there under trees. Not bad. My sister seemed to like the school most of the time and only once in a while cried when we left after a visit.

Inside it looked okay too, although the whole place smelled like the stuff our cleaning lady, Mrs. Shrub, uses to clean the bathroom, and once when I just wanted to get some fresh air and tried to open a window, the window let out alarm screams like the phantom of the opera and people came running from every direction like I'd set the place on fire.

Most of the rooms were big, with beds in rows and a bunch of lockers at one end, and a TV set and a chair in the corner for the guard. The guard sat there all night to make sure everybody slept. My mother said not to call the guard a guard. The guard was an attendant, she said.

Anyway, the attendant told us my sister was in the dining room having lunch and we would have to wait, and my father asked if it would be all right if we went into the dining room to see if she was finished. The attendant said it was against regulations, and when he said that, he sounded like a guard, not like an attendant.

So we sat on my sister's bed and waited and waited, and my father kept looking at his watch and finally he said it was getting late and he didn't want to get into heavy traffic and why didn't we just walk in the direction of the dining room and peek in and wave at my sister to hurry up?

My mother knew the way. We went through a lot of empty corridors and one that wasn't empty. An attendant was wheeling a sleeping person in a wheelchair and talking to him at the same time. I couldn't figure out why he was talking to someone asleep until we came up close, and then I saw that the man in the chair wasn't sleeping at all. His neck was just bent down like that, his head resting on his shirt as if he were trying to push his chin into his pocket. And he was wide awake and looking at us, especially at me. When we passed the chair, the man never moved, but his eyes just followed us as we went by. He had very fierce, dark eyebrows over staring eyes, but I pretended not to notice, because my mother had warned me about a hundred times to expect to see people behave in ways that might seem peculiar but not to embarrass anybody by bugging out my eyes and staring or asking, "What's wrong with *him?*"

My mother said that even if the people here had been doled out a little less smartness, it didn't mean they had any less feelings.

The dining room was in the next building, so we had to go outside. We passed a fenced-in area where a group of girls were sitting in a circle on the ground and doing what looked like exercises with a leader. One of the girls was lying outside the circle flat down with her face smack in the grass, and another girl was racing along the fence, grabbing it here and there and waving to us. I remembered what my mother had said about people's feelings, and I waved back.

The dining room door had two portholes. They were too high for me to see into, but not too high for my father. We were about to go in and just wave at my sister to hurry up, when my dad suddenly said, "I don't think we should," and he stopped dead and turned his back to the door. I guess he'd just taken a peek and changed his mind. I thought that was funny since it had been his idea in the first place, and I guess my mother thought it was strange too, because she just looked at him without saying much and then suggested she take just one step inside alone and see if she could find my sister.

"I want to go too," I said. I guess I was curious to see if it was anything like our school cafeteria, but the minute we stepped inside, I knew it was a lot different.

Almost immediately a lady jumped out from nowhere and blocked our way. Her hair was the same ghost white as her uniform. "I'm sorry, no guests are allowed in the dining room," she said. She sounded like my old fourth-grade teacher, Miss Drummond, who'd had a voice like the loud notes on an electric organ.

"We're just here to—" my mother started to say, but the lady had each of us by one elbow and was trying to turn us right around so we wouldn't see what was going on.

I only had a glimpse and I'm not sure my mother saw what I saw, but right away I figured this dining hall was one reason my mother wanted my sister to come home to live.

All the kids were wearing the same big white

bibs marked "Green Valley Regional Training Center," and they were all eating off plastic plates. They didn't have knives or forks though, just little spoons. And everybody was eating the same thing—no kidding—baby food. On every plate was a little orange pile of baby food and a little grey pile of what looked like the same stuff. There were older people here too, some who looked older than my father, and they were wearing bibs and eating baby food too. Some were being forced to eat it. Attendants were holding their jaws open and spooning it into their mouths. I saw my mother turn her head away and I didn't much want to look either, so we allowed ourselves to be ushered right out again the way we'd come, but not before I'd seen that a lot of the people there, seated at the long tables, were tied into their chairs with heavy leather straps.

To save time, we decided to open my sister's locker and pack her things into the suitcase before she returned. The attendant came and opened her locker and we took out her stuff: a little bunch of clothes, four crayons, papers with her drawings, a flashlight without a battery, part of a tea set my mother had given her on her birthday, and a Christmas card I'd sent her two years ago.

My mother called the attendant after she'd put everything in the suitcase. "Where are the rest of my daughter's things?" she asked.

"Is anything missing?" the attendant asked. He

was yawning, maybe from having to stay up all night watching everybody else sleep.

"But this can't be all! I sent my daughter a little radio just two weeks ago! And what happened to her drawing pad and the big box of pastels? Where are the picture books and the lacing cards? Where are the rest of her *clothes?*"

The attendant shrugged. "Things get stolen here all the time," he said.

My mother's face turned very red. She looked at my father. My father took her arm. "Forget it," he said. "It's all over." He looked into the large suitcase we'd expected to fill and then at my sister's things, which were bunched up in one small pile, and he didn't say another word. My mother shook her head and looked down at the floor while he closed the bag and set it at the foot of the bed.

The girl who sleeps in the bed next to my sister got back from lunch first, and I didn't know whether I was supposed to say hello and pretend I hadn't noticed the contraption on her head or just look down at the floor and act as if I hadn't seen her at all. I was really scared for a minute; if they had to keep her head in a cage like that, was she maybe dangerous?

But she just laughed and said hello like any other person would and we all said, "How are you?" and the attendant came over and unstrapped her cage so she could lie down and take a rest. The cage actually looked like the white skeleton of a football helmet with a chin strap. The girl lay down on her bed and I noticed the bed had sides, like a crib; there were also rubber pads all around on the floor, in case she fell out anyway. Later, my mother whispered to me that the girl often had seizures and the helmet protected her if she fell suddenly to the floor. She explained that seizures are blackouts that happen very suddenly and without warning.

Other kids started coming in from lunch and pretty soon the dormitory was almost full, except for my sister.

My mother and father kept staring at the door, wishing my sister would hurry, anxious to leave, but I knew why she was going to be the last one in, for sure. She is not that fast at walking and has a funny step, as if she never quite got the hang of putting one foot in front of the other. Her toes point in towards each other and it's almost as if she's learning a new dance routine and wants to get it really right. Step/step, step/step.

In she came at last and sure enough, she was the next-to-last kid back from lunch. She stepped in and I took one look and my mouth flew open. Of course, I hadn't seen her for quite a while, not since last Christmas, but good, grey grief! What had they done to her, anyway?

two

MY SISTER'S NAME IS GERALDINE, AFTER MY GRAND-
father, Gerald Oxley, who was famous. Well, not
exactly famous, but he did play with the American
Piano Quartet on the radio in 1944, and had his
picture in the newspapers quite a lot when he en-
tertained troops during the Second World War. He
was my father's father and he died before I was
born, but my father liked him a lot and still keeps
his picture in a frame right up on the piano, next
to mine.

My father takes after my grandfather too. He
has perfect pitch and plays really well, although he
is not a professional musician; he is a stockbroker,
but he can do fantastic things with the keyboard,
and he writes songs. He wrote "You Put the Oh in
Love" and a rock group almost made a record of it
for RCA last year, but the deal fell through.

My father wants me to play too, and I try, but

my fingers seem to slip a lot and hit the wrong keys, although Mrs. Reinhardt, my piano teacher, says where there's life, there's a possibility of a Mozart.

Geraldine was born a year before I was, and at first they thought she was okay. Pretty soon, though, my mother noticed that Gerri couldn't suck her breast enough to get milk and when she cried, she sounded more like a toy you wind up with a key than a baby. She wasn't getting any bigger, either. When it was time to take Geraldine home from the hospital, she'd gotten smaller instead of larger. The doctors agreed she was impaired but couldn't agree on why. My mother told me that Gerri's condition was no easier to explain than it was to explain a birthmark. So Gerri, who was born damaged, stayed on at the hospital and my mother came home.

Geraldine didn't grow for a long time. After she did begin to grow, she could never learn to hold up her own head. My mother said if she didn't hold it up for her, it would flop right over like a flower in a downpour. Later, when other babies were sitting up, Geraldine just lay in her crib. She couldn't turn over and she couldn't seem to learn to hold things in her hands, or to laugh. My mother wanted to bring her home, but she got pregnant with me then and people started giving her advice. My mother says she's had so much advice she's gotten allergic to it; she says it makes her itch. Everybody told my mother to put Geraldine into a home where she'd be better off, and my father said, "Do whatever you think is best," and so Geraldine was put into the Roxbury School, which was closed down after two years for health violations, and then she was sent to the Woodstream Academy, which was very good but went bankrupt, and then the Lower River School, which was too overcrowded, and finally my parents had to send her here, to the Green Valley Regional Training Center, which is so far away we rarely got to see her. My mother said the Woodstream Academy had been better. One thing is sure: in all the years we'd been coming on holidays and long weekends, we'd never seen Geraldine looking like this!

I heard my mother gasp. My father turned white around his moustache. He said to the attendant, "What's happened to Gerri? Why does she look like that?"

The side of my sister's head was blue-black and there was a bump over her ear. What was even worse was that where the bump was sticking out, hair was missing, as if it had been pulled out by the handful or shaved clean off her head, leaving just a few wisps that couldn't cover the bulge.

The attendant and my parents moved off into the attendant's corner and got into a huddle; whatever it was that had torn the hair out of my sister's head was going to be super hush-hush, judging by the way they were whispering, looking her way and nodding. It was like they wanted to keep the secret right in that corner, like a wrecked piece of furniture.

As awful as her head looked, it didn't seem to bother Gerri. All this time she was holding on to my sleeve, or running over to pick up the suitcase and set it down again, or coming back and hugging me and wrapping her arms around my arm. You would think with all the moves she'd made, she'd be used to it. Or did she understand she was coming home? Geraldine has this funny laugh that sounds like it's climbing a ladder, up and up, higher and higher, like *ho, ha, hee,* and then *YEE!* She was talking too, but when Gerri talks, no one understands what she is saying because—no kidding—the words all come out sounding like she's reciting the names of Santa Claus's reindeer: Dasha, Dansa, Donda, Blitzen—like that.

Sometimes, between words, Gerri forgets to close her mouth and just leaves it open. That's when she looks all wrong and funny; otherwise, when her hair is combed right, she looks pretty much like every other kid and a lot prettier than some of the girls in my class. Her top teeth are crooked, but mine were too, until I got braces, and although my father doesn't think it's necessary to put Gerri through all that trouble, my mother says she hopes we'll be able to get Gerri a toothpaste smile exactly like mine.

I couldn't help noticing that the girl in the next bed wasn't sleeping at all. She was watching us through the metal protecting bars, just lying there, not moving, not speaking.

When it was time to go, my father lifted the suitcase and held out his hand. "Come on, Gerri," he said. "Time to leave."

Gerri opened her mouth and stared, not moving.

"Come on, let's go," Dad said. He took a step in her direction and Gerri backed up and moved away from him.

"Hey, what's wrong?" Dad said.

Gerri made a sound in her throat. It sounded like "Donner" or "Donde" or "Dahnda." You could see her tongue moving in her mouth, like it was trying to find the right place to land. "Dahanda, dahan."

My mother rushed over to put her arm around Gerri. She pulled her very close. "What's wrong? Don't you want to come with us?"

"Dhanda." Gerri's mouth stayed open. It was wet in one corner. She'd backed right up against a locker.

"My mother turned to me. "Neil, can you understand her? What is she saying?"

I didn't know. She could have been talking Czechoslovakian for all I was getting.

The girl in the next bed all of a sudden pulled herself up on the steel protecting bars and pointed to my father. "His moustache," she said. "She's scared of it."

"Of course!" my mother cried, sounding very relieved, and we all had a laugh. When Gerri saw everybody laughing, she joined in, and little by little Dad got closer and closer to her until she finally let him take her hand and move it up under his nose to feel the brushy new hair. Gerri's laugh went higher and higher and then she said, "Tash." I heard it and Mom heard it and Mom said, "Hey, I think Gerri said 'moustache,'" but when we asked her to say "moustache" again, she said, "Blixen."

More weird words came out of her when she saw that we were going to get into the car. She'd been for a few automobile rides, but she didn't get to go very often. I guess she felt about our old blue "ord" (the F has been missing off the back for about five years) the way I feel about roller coasters: that's how her voice sounded as she climbed in, like oh-boy-here-it-comes! Then for the first half-hour she never shut up; it was like having a tape recorder sitting right there next to me on the back seat. I even saw my father look over at my mother and smile a couple of times, and when we passed the cows we'd passed coming up, out came the old *ha-hee-hi-YEE*, with Gerri pointing out the window and bouncing in her seat like she was sitting on a spring.

Then, O gross, no warning, she just got quiet for a couple of minutes, put her head down, and threw up. Just like that.

Dad pulled off the highway and drove a few minutes until we found a gas station, and while my mother walked Gerri in the fresh air to clear her head, Dad and I went to the men's room to get some paper towels and to fill our thermos with water for the cleanup, and Dad all of a sudden turned to me and said, "Neil, it's not going to be easy," and I thought he was talking about cleaning up the back of the car and I said, "I know." But later, when we finally got home and had that awful scene in the elevator, I realized Dad wasn't only talking about the mess in our car.

Dad was trying to warn me about what it was going to be like living with Gerri.

three

I'M GOING TO BE HONEST AND COME RIGHT OUT AND
say it: I don't like school. It's not that the place itself is bad; to look at it you'd say it was pretty
nice, modern and bright, with red carpets and
green blackboards. What's bum about the school,
aside from some of the lunches they serve in the
cafeteria, is the kids. It's not even that the kids
aren't nice either, it's that they come in bunches,
like grapes. There's the jock bunch, and they all
hang out together near the gym, and then there's
the East End bunch, who all live in the same hous-
ing development and cluster upstairs in the corridor, and there are the brains and they flock
together near the math office. There's also the
music and drama set, who all clump together near
the auditorium. When they aren't huddled in these
places, they sit together in the cafeteria or outside

on the steps. Where do I fit in? That's the problem. I am not a jock, not an East-Ender, not a brain, and not a music/drama person. I like to take pictures and paste them in albums or fool around at the piano or just fool around; what's more, I'm sort of new. All the kids at Franklin Pierce Junior High came either from Remington Elementary or Lady of Mercy Parochial School.

I came from private school, and that, to the kids, is like I'm from the North Star. I didn't know any of the kids everyone else knew and I didn't know any of the teachers and I had a different way of doing math and I had read all the wrong books; like I said, practically like coming from a secondary planet. Half the time I wished I were back in private school where my friends are, but when my mother decided to have Geraldine come home to live, she had to give up her job and we couldn't afford the tuition.

I shouldn't say I have *no* friends in school. I have one friend, Joe Newbolt, who is in the music/drama group and wants to have his name changed to Jason Newley. He thinks a name like Joe Newbolt is not good for his image and now wants everyone to call him Jason. Half the time I forget and Joe/Jason gets mad, so we have our ups and downs, but he's someone I talk to.

When I told him Geraldine was coming home to live, he gasped. He practices gasping for theater a lot, and does it really well. "Watch out," he gasped, "just watch out." Then a minute later he said he really dug the name Geraldine—it had a tragic ring. Finally, he said, "Well, it should be a real trip, Neil-boy," and I couldn't help remembering those very words when we first took Gerri up in the elevator.

We live on the sixth floor, so with or without her suitcase it was never a question of walking up, although we should have been smart enough to realize that a first ride in the elevator for Gerri might seem like a parachute jump for anyone else. The funny thing was that she was gung ho to get on and followed Dad right in without hesitation. What happened, unfortunately, was that in addition to Dad, Mom, me, and Gerri, there were two other people on board: Mr. Rasmussen from the fifth floor with his Scottie dog, and Miss Gropper from the fourth. Just as the elevator door began to close, another person, the delivery boy from the nursery, carrying a tree in a tub, squeezed in. The doors closed and the delivery boy pushed the button for the seventh floor. Dad had pushed six, of course, and Mr. Rasmussen had pushed five. Miss Gropper had pushed four.

I guess Gerri, watching everyone press a floor button, figured that it was a requirement of all elevator riders to push a button; before anyone knew enough to stop her, she reached over and pressed the most colorful, eye-catching, brightest of all the buttons—the one clearly marked EMERGENCY.

Immediately an alarm went off that sounded as

if it were signaling the end of all life on earth, a scream of an alarm that must have been heard by the dead and the deaf, a shriek that felt like it could put a hole right through the side of the building. The button had jammed. Geraldine went wild. I guess she realized she'd made a mistake, and went to correct it. She leaped forward to push another button to try to make up for the goof and—no kidding—it turned off the lights and stopped the elevator dead with a jerk somewhere between two floors.

Gerri began to jump and scream, scream and jump, and was immediately joined by Mr. Rasmussen's Scottie, who started to yelp. Mr. Rasmussen is nervous (as I later found out) and tried to outscream Gerri, the alarm, and his dog. He was not just screaming screams, he was screaming words, but I didn't quite catch them. I think one of them was *Help*.

Miss Gropper is a heavy-type lady, with the sort of body that seems to fill up clothes and the sort of arms that use up whole sleeves. She began slapping the walls and making sounds like you might hear coming out of an orchestra pit when the violinists are tuning up. My father kept saying, "Calm! Stay calm!" but his voice sounded like someone was trying to push him off a cliff, and just hearing his voice come out so high took all the breath out of me. My mother sounded like she was practicing reciting the vowels. She was saying

"Aah, oh, eee, ooo." I could hardly breathe I was so scared. Was the elevator hanging there by a thread? Were we all going to plunge into the sub-basement and end up as a pile of broken bodies and bones in the cellar or just explode into bits in mid-air?

Finally my father (or someone) turned the lights back on. First thing I saw was the delivery boy holding his neck with both his hands, crouching in the corner behind his tree, looking as if he were waiting for death. Mr. Rasmussen, who had picked up his dog and was holding him under one arm, was hanging on to Miss Gropper with the other. Miss Gropper was hanging on to Geraldine, who was looking straight up and still screaming her head off.

Suddenly, the siren stopped. My mother had punched it with her fist and it turned itself off. The elevator wobbled and started up, shaking only slightly on its way to the fourth floor.

Miss Gropper, wiping her left eye with a tissue, was helped off. On her way out I heard her say, "Those kinds of children should not be allowed on elevators!" but I don't think my mother or father heard. Mr. Rasmussen, with my father's help, his head and body shaking like he was treading water, got off with his dog on the fifth floor. He said a bad word just as the doors closed behind him.

Gerri had calmed down, but my mother and father had to help her out of the elevator. She was breathing very hard, taking big, loud gasps, the very opposite of me, who was still hardly getting any air in my lungs at all. I kept thinking that if this was a sample of what life with my sister was going to be like, we were probably making a monster mistake.

four

My mother was looking worried too, and I saw her holding Gerri's hand tight while my father opened the door to the apartment. Actually, I don't think she needed to, because the minute the door opened, Gerri calmed right down as if she were about to step into a museum or a church or someplace where you had to be really quiet. My mother took her right through the living room and I followed them; I was really anxious to see what Gerri would do when she saw her own room.

My mother had put my old stuffed rag doll, Woodie, on the bed (Woodie has the vest with the buttons and buttonholes and laces that taught me how to tie a bow), and Geraldine made a beeline for it and laughed and said "Blixen," or something like that, and then she just lay down on the bed and hugged and hugged the doll and held it like somebody was going to try to take it away from her. My mother looked at me with this funny look like she was going to laugh with one side of her mouth and cry with the other side, but then she just smiled and put her hand on my shoulder. I guess she'd decided right there and then that elevator disasters or no, having Gerri home was going to be worth it.

My father was standing in the new doorway and smiling too.

"She seems to like it here, doesn't she?" he said.

Gerri had noticed the flowers on the window sill and was already on her way to examine them. "Smell them, Gerri," my mother said, and Gerri put her face right smack into the vase and practically knocked it over trying to breathe in the perfume. "Dasha," Gerri said and she inhaled again. I'd never seen anybody in my life who appreciated flowers that much, or for that matter, everything. My mother showed her the chest of drawers full of her new clothes and the wicker chest she'd filled with some of my old picture books and a xylophone with a little hammer and a top that never really worked right. Everything—bedroom slippers, comb and brush, wooden bank shaped like a train—went over very, very big, like we were giving her the lost treasure of the Incas or something.

She liked the Welcome Home cake too, although—believe it or not—she didn't seem to know what it was for. The minute my mother took it out of the refrigerator Gerri looked like she was going to make a dive for it with both hands. It looked beautiful and I could see which way she was heading right off, but luckily my father saw the look in her eyes too, and got to the cake just in time. He pulled it out of her reach and said, "No, no, Gerri, we *eat* this!" and he cut her a nice big piece with a cake cutter and put it on a plate for her and set it down on the table. My mother gave Gerri a fork and tried to show her how to use it, and Gerri sat down at the table and oh, good, grey grief, she couldn't eat the cake.

I mean, she couldn't get a piece speared on the fork. And when my mother had helped get the cake and fork together, Gerri couldn't seem to aim it towards her mouth. My mother said, "They've never really taught her to feed herself properly, Ted," and my father nodded. Then, with my mother's help, once she got it into her mouth, she didn't really get the hang of how to chew it.

"I'll unpack her things, Margery," my father said, and I said I'd go help him put her suitcase away. I guess neither of us wanted to watch Gerri learn how to eat.

In fact, when we got back from putting Gerri's suitcase in the basement storage room, my mother was still wiping up the mess in the kitchen; there was whipped cream everyplace you wanted to look. There was even a little whipped cream on my mother's forehead, but my mother was smiling. "Gerri loved the cake," she said.

"But wait until you try to give her carrots," my

father said, smiling, and he disappeared into the living room, while my mother was still sponging the floor. She'd given Gerri a sponge too, and Gerri was helping, if you can call waxing the floor with whipped cream helping.

Every evening when he comes home from work, my father plays the piano. He usually practices scales, then he runs through some of the pieces he's written. He hums along with the music with his head to one side (as though he can concentrate better if his head is tilted) and sometimes he sort of half closes his eyes like he's trying to remember which note comes next, or maybe he's thinking of something altogether different, like who won the Spanish-American War or what we're going to have for dinner. He says he has to play to relax and when he plays I'm not allowed to disturb him unless it's a real emergency, like the bathtub overflowing or a stove fire.

Tonight, the minute the sound of the very first note came plinking into the kitchen, Geraldine went absolutely zonkers. She dropped the sponge and sat smack on the wet floor and threw her head back and said, "Eee! Donneh, donneh."

Then she was dead quiet for a long time listening. My mother winked at me. "Looks like your sister likes music, Neil."

It did look that way. She shuffle-shuffled into the living room and pulled a chair next to the piano and climbed aboard, like it was the back of a pickup truck and she was going on a hayride. She just plumped herself up there and crossed her legs and tilted her head to one side like my father's, and just sat up there smiling her head off.

My father had stopped playing, of course, and just sat there staring as if he couldn't believe his eyes. "What's going on?" he said.

"Gerri seems to like your playing a lot," my mother said, coming out of the kitchen smiling, the whipped cream still on her head.

"Listen, she can't sit on the piano," my father said. He wasn't smiling a bit.

"Geraldine, get off the piano," my mother said.

Even though his moustache was hiding his mouth, I could tell my father was annoyed. My dad loves his piano. It's a big Bechstein, and no kidding, it's the size and color of a hippopotamus when it comes out of the water at the zoo. It was my grandfather's and is a hundred years old, but it plays great. It takes up a big corner of our living room and my mother said that when we moved in, they couldn't get it into the elevators and had to pull it through the windows on pulleys and ropes, in pieces. To my father, his piano is like something behind glass at a museum, like priceless. He never even opens it, because he doesn't want the dust to float into it and mess up the strings, and he won't let my mother put wax on it, either. He doesn't trust wax any more than he trusts dust.

Geraldine got the message right off; she could tell she'd goofed by my Dad's tone and climbed right off the piano, but not before she'd knocked the picture of my grandfather to the floor on her way down. The glass luckily didn't break or anything, but my dad jumped up and rushed to pick it up and examine it for cracks.

"She didn't mean it, Ted," my mother said, helping Gerri down. "Tell Daddy you're sorry, Gerri," my mother said, and Gerri said, "Vixen, vixxxen."

My dad was now looking over the piano, trying to find scratches. Gerri said, "Vixen, blixen," but my father didn't pay any attention. He was too busy running his finger back and forth along a little mark he'd found along the edge.

"I think she apologized, Ted," my mother said, and my dad finally looked up.

"I know she didn't mean it, Margery," he said and then he said, "You have whipped cream on your forehead, did you know it?" but he still looked serious.

My mother wiped the cream off her forehead with the back of her wrist and said, "I think I'll give Gerri something warm to drink and put her to bed. She's exhausted," and she took Gerri by the hand and led her back to the kitchen, which is where we were now eating since we had given Gerri the dining room.

My father sat back on the piano bench and looked at me.

"I'm tired too, Neil," he said. "Really tired. Aren't you?"

"I guess so," I said.

"It's been quite a day," he said, and he struck up a minor key chord and closed his eyes. "Quite a day," he said, sort of to himself. I just sat on the sofa and listened to him play, but I should have gone right to bed. I didn't know that within a few hours I'd find out what had made the bumpy-bald mess out of my sister's head.

It had been quite a day. It was going to be quite a night too.

five

I WENT TO BED BEFORE TEN WITH THE IDEA OF READ-
ing one chapter of the book I'm supposed to do a
report on for English, but I hardly got through one
page. I didn't know if it's that I'm just not that interested in spear-fishing in Canada or if the long
trip to Geraldine's school wore me out, but I could
hardly stay awake long enough to reach over and
switch off the light next to my bed.

When you're sleeping, time gets all mixed up,
so I couldn't say whether I'd been lying there for
hours or whether I'd just fallen off to sleep, but I
do know that one minute I was sleeping and the
next minute I was as wide awake as morning, as if
my alarm had gone off. Only it hadn't gone off at
all, and the digital dial, when I could get my eyes
into the right focus, was glowing 1:08.

The funny thing is that I woke up scared, as if
something was going to happen, or had already

happened. It was dark as a cave in my room, probably because my mother had forgotten to leave on the bathroom light, and the digital numbers 1:09, 1:10, 1:11 threw just enough of a gold-green glow to remind me of the Night of the Living Dead.

Then! A sudden, hard thump—the sort of sound a fist would make striking a . . . well, a coffin—and again, the same, hard, scary knock, coming from very nearby.

I waited, not daring to move or to scream. The knock came again, then again, in a repeating hollow drum rhythm: *BLAM BLAM BLAM BLAM*. Was someone trying to break into the apartment, smash in the special dead-bolt locks my father had put on the front door after the neighbors were robbed last year?

Then I remembered Gerri. The room my parents had enclosed for her was next to mine. Was Gerri making these cemetery noises in the dead of night? What in the name of the avenging spirit was going on at 1:12, 1:13, 1:14 A.M. in her room?

I didn't bother with slippers. With my heart going in my chest like somebody had cranked it up, I tiptoed through the black hall to the kitchen. Now I discovered why my mother hadn't left a light in the bathroom: she'd left the small one over the stove on in the kitchen instead. It shone directly into Gerri's room, and was probably supposed to keep her from getting scared if she woke up in the middle of the night. I guess they didn't figure *I* might wake up and die of fright, but it now seemed like a good possibility.

I peered into Gerri's room until my eyes got used to the dim-dark, trying to get my bearings and preparing myself for who-knows-what waiting in there for me.

Who-knows-what turned out to be my sister, all right. Gerri was kneeling on her bed, slamming her head into the wall—*BLAM BRAM BLAM BRAM*—like it was a normal, everyday thing everybody did in the middle of the night.

"Geraldine! Stop it!" I said. I admit I was really shook. What was she trying to do? Knock herself unconscious? Put holes in the plaster? No wonder the hair was worn thin on her head. No wonder she had that big, fat welty bump on her head.

"Stop it!" I said again. "Will you please cut it out!"

But it would have been easier reasoning with a ghost in a sheet. She just kept right on, *BRAM BRAM BRAM*, like she had a quota of crashes to fill and didn't want to be interrupted.

Was she determined to wake everybody in the world, let alone this building? Just when I was trying to decide whether this fell into the category of the same sort of emergency as overflowing bathtubs that justified waking my mother, she came running in.

"Gerri!" she said, "Oh, Gerri!"

She ran over to my sister and sat on the bed and threw her arms around her and held her head against her shoulder and started rocking her, rock-abye-baby style, and saying "Gerri, Gerri," and humming off-key. It was something to see, my mother holding someone Gerri's size practically on her lap, but it seemed to calm Gerri right down. Gerri started to hum too, but I guess it was a different tune from my mother's, because it sounded awful.

I think it was Gerri's humming that finally woke my father.

He came shuffling in, his eyelids looking pasted together, the belt from his robe trailing behind him on the floor. "Hey, what's going on here?" he said, but his voice sounded as if it were coming from another floor.

"Everything's all right now, Ted," my mother said, still rocking, interrupting her humming for a minute. "Problem's solved."

"What'd she do?" my father said, coming a little more awake, but not much.

"You know, the head-banging thing," my mother sort of whispered.

Why she was whispering I couldn't figure out since it was certainly no secret that my sister had practically put a hole in the pink wall and would have put her head right through the bricks if we hadn't come running in to save her and the apartment.

My father nodded as if it were the most natural thing for someone to wake up at one in the morning and work out against the plaster.

"Why does she do that?" I asked. I heard myself whispering too.

My mother gave me sort of a high sign over Gerri's head, like we wouldn't discuss it in her presence but she'd tell me later. Dad put his arm around my shoulder and walked back to my room with me. He put me under the covers, which he hasn't done since I had my tonsils and adenoids out, and sat on the edge of my blanket. A minute later my mother came in and sat next to him, and my dad said, "I hope your sister didn't upset you, doing that?" and my mother said that it was a little scary but not to be worried. I wasn't frightened, was I? And I said I wasn't, but why did she want to do that, *hurt* herself like that?

My mother sighed and looked at my father, and he was just playing with the cord of his pajamas and looking at nothing, and my mother said that it was just a way that Gerri had of trying to beat the frustrations out—like some people might kick a ball real hard or jog until they fell down exhausted.

"Gerri can't do what most children her age can do," my mother said. "It upsets her. And when she speaks and we don't understand her, it frustrates her terribly. And when she can't walk right or catch a ball or eat a piece of cake, and when people laugh at her—*especially* when people laugh at her, or run away from her—it's like there's a hard knot of unhappiness she can't untie—and believe it or not, banging her head, even when she feels the hurt, makes her feel better."

I understood, but I didn't really want to understand. Long after my parents left me alone in my room, long after everything was peaceful and still, I turned it over in my mind. I tried not to think about how it would be to be Geraldine, how it would feel to be spending your first night with your own family instead of being one person in a room filled with rows of beds and a guard, how it must have been to call for your mother at night at the top of your voice, even scream for her when everything was black and still, and know all the time she'd never come and that only the guard, who didn't care at all, would hear you.

I just lay there in bed and every now and then I looked at the glowy numbers of my digital clock: 2:46, 2:47, 2:48. No kidding, I just couldn't get to sleep. For the longest time, I couldn't seem to get my own knots untied.

Finally, though, I did fall asleep and I had the weirdest dream. I dreamed I found a diamond the size of a light bulb under my desk during old lady Bowring's English class. Wow, it weighed a ton and it had a shine like Christmas and in my dream it made me like the rajah of the school. Everybody wanted to be my friend.

What a letdown when I woke up. I was back to being just me, diamondless, no rajah, and pretty much alone as usual. But there was a surprise waiting for me, and believe it or not, it did happen in old lady Bowring's English class, fourth period.

six

IT IS SAID AROUND SCHOOL THAT MRS. BOWRING WAS born around the turn of the century but that nobody can figure out which century. I guess she must have been a good teacher once when her systems were all in working order, but lately she can't see or hear beyond the third row. If you're lucky and manage to get a seat in the fourth or, better still, the fifth or sixth row, it's like having a free period. Some of the best fights at school are fought over the back seats in Bowring's class, and nobody is ever late for English, because aside from a couple of the brains, everyone whizzes into her room way ahead of time to be sure to get the farthest seats from her desk.

Which is where Joe/Jason and I have most of our conversations.

Today, while Bowring plodded through Canadian spear-fishing, Joe/Jason and I played a couple of games of Dots and Tic-Tac-Toe, and I decorated my notebook with the flags of the world, which I have pretty well memorized.

All of a sudden, Joe/Jason whispered, "Say, you know how to play the piano, don't you, Neil?"

I never know how to answer a question like that because I can play "Country Gardens" and two Chopin études pretty well and I can play "Happy Birthday to You" like a virtuoso, but if you want to hear anything else, better call my father or look in the Yellow Pages under Piano Players because even if it's easy, I'll sure as anything botch it.

"Not too good," I said, and I put the finishing touches on a real good Greek flag in the corner of my book.

"Listen, we need a piano player for the Franklin Pierce Follies," Joe/Jason said.

"Count me out, Joe," I said, and he gave me a killer-look. "Count me out, *Jason*, I mean," I said.

"Listen, Neil, don't be a dummy," Joe/Jason said. "It just means learning a couple of easy pieces and playing with the band. It's like this: The band does most of the work, and every once in a while, like for emphasis, the band stops and you go *Plink Plink Plink*. It's not Tchaikovsky, sweetheart."

"Forget it," I said. "Blot it right out of your head. Anyhow, what's the Franklin Pierce Follies?"

"A big show the drama group is putting on. Come on, Neil, if you hit a couple of wrong keys, is the world gonna stop turning? Who'll know the difference if you get a plink or two wrong?"

He had me and he knew he had me; if I got involved in the Franklin Pierce Follies, maybe I'd work my way into the drama bunch, which wouldn't exactly turn me into a rajah but might get me out of this singles act. Also, the drama kids are not a bad bunch, actually.

Old lady Bowring was looking in our direction, or at least her glasses seemed to be aimed at us. "Keep a low profile," Joe/Jason whispered, "and think it over. You can start working on the Battle Hymn of the Republic and I'll get the rest of the music to you as soon as I can."

"You call the Battle Hymn of the Republic *Plink Plink Plink?*" I said.

"Shhh. You can do it!" Joe/Jason whispered.

I admit I flew home right after school and started exercising my fingers, doing scales and chords and tearing the place apart looking through every old songbook for the Battle Hymn of the Republic. I found it in a book mixed in with Christmas carols and the Brahms Lullaby: it had lots of sharps and flats and might impress whoever was supposed to be in charge of tryouts if I could get it right, no easy job.

My mother and Gerri were out at the park, according to Mrs. Shrub our cleaning lady, so this should have been a nice quiet time to play, but no luck. Mrs. Shrub brought the upright vacuum cleaner into the living room and planted it smack next to the coffee table, not so she could vacuum, but so she could lean on it and complain about her back, which hurts her a lot down on the right side. So instead of practicing, I sat on the piano bench and listened to Mrs. Shrub's health problems and also answered a lot of questions about Geraldine that Mrs. Shrub probably didn't like asking my mother. And every time I answered a question about my sister, Mrs. Shrub said, "Poor thing," and shook her head and then quick thought up another question. Finally, when Mrs. Shrub heard my mother's key in the lock she remembered she hadn't cleaned the bedroom and disappeared, dragging the vacuum behind her.

My mother was too tired to be surprised to see me practicing the piano of my own free will and just flopped down on the couch and took her shoes off. Gerri, hearing the vacuum going in the bedroom, shuffled off; my mother said Gerri had been trying to help Mrs. Shrub clean all morning, and she added, "Poor thing." She meant Mrs. Shrub.

Then my mother told me that she was exhausted after her outing with Gerri because Gerri was now afraid of the elevator and my mother had to walk down six flights on the way out and walk up six flights on the way back. She also said Gerri has a habit of going up to perfect strangers and just throwing her arms around them and hugging them. Before my mother could stop her she had hugged two old ladies, an ice-cream vendor, and a sleeping bum, and we were going to have to start teaching Gerri to shake hands before we all got into a lot of trouble . . .

CRASHO. My mother and I looked at each other; the sound and Mrs. Shrub's voice could be heard traveling through the apartment air like a Chinese gong. *"Geraldine!"*

My mother and I jumped up, prepared for the worst, and there it was in the bedroom. Gerri had pulled down my mother's big, fancy draperies, complete with rods, tassels, and rings. They were lying there on the floor in a big messy heap under the bare window, making the whole room look like we'd fought a war in it.

My mother said, "Oh, Gerri!" and I could see Gerri was scared; she had her mouth open and was backing into the corner where my father keeps his clothing valet; was she afraid my mother was going to *hit* her?

My mother reached over to try to stop the valet from going over and Gerri got so scared, probably thinking my mother was going to grab her, that she let out a couple of shrieks that sounded like dawn in the jungle. Just then my father stepped into the bedroom. With all the commotion, no-body'd even heard him come home.

His face looked like it didn't believe what it was seeing. "What's happening here?" he said, and he had to say it a couple of times before anybody really heard him, because of the noises Gerri was making.

"The little girl pulled down the curtains," Mrs. Shrub said, meaning Gerri, who is taller than she is. She was shaking her head and looking very sad, as if someone had died.

"Why did she do *that?*" my father asked.

My mother still had her hand on the wobbling valet. "I think maybe she was watching Mrs. Shrub pull the sheets off the bed and got mixed up. She's never seen a room with curtains before, Ted. There were no curtains at the home. She might think they don't belong on the windows."

My father shook his head. "I think I'll go have a drink," he said and then he stopped, turned to me, and said, "Want to come to the kitchen with me, Neil, keep me company?"

"I thought I'd go in, practice the piano for a while," I said. My father's mouth flew open under his moustache, and no kidding, just then he looked a lot like Gerri. I never noticed until that minute that they had practically the same nose and the same shape head, only his bald spot is on top. "You're going in to *practice the piano?* Without anybody putting even the slightest squeeze on you? Or is this April Fool, Neil?"

I had to tell him then about the Franklin Pierce Follies tryouts and you should have seen how excited he got. He forgot all about the draperies and the drink and flew right over to the piano and sat on the bench and patted the place next to him and said, "Come on, Neil, we'll work on this every night until we get it right," and then we had to get up so he could shuffle through the music we keep in the piano bench to find a simpler version of the Battle Hymn of the Republic, which he finally found in a book of patriotic songs. He put it on the music stand and turned on the metronome and began to play it very slowly so I could follow what he was doing with his left hand, and sure enough, he hadn't played two bars before Gerri appeared and one, two, three, she had dragged over a chair and was climbing up on the piano again. My father had to stop and say, "Geraldine, get off!" and rescue the photo of Grandpa that was wobbling and ready to fall.

Which is when the doorbell rang.

I was in no mood to have anybody come into our apartment and see my father trying to get my sister off the piano and to hear the commotion from the bedroom where my mother and Mrs. Shrub were trying to rehang the draperies, but the doorbell rang again and I had to answer it.

If I'd known who was coming to see me, I wouldn't have opened the door at all. I would have pretended we were all out or asleep or didn't want to be disturbed, but of course, I had no idea who was waiting out in the hall.

"I'm coming!" I called, and I looked through the peephole that lets us check out visitors to make sure they're not crooks, and no kidding, I had to look twice to make sure I was seeing right. Oh, good, grey grief, what was *he* doing here, anyway?

seven

My mother had heard the doorbell too, and was almost behind me when I opened the door. "What are *you* doing here, Joe?" I said.

"Jason, Jason, Jason, for crying out loud!" said Joe/Jason. "I brought you the sheet music, for the tryouts. What are friends for, baby?"

I had the door open just a crack so Joe/Jason couldn't look into the apartment. "Thanks," I said, and I took the music and tried to close the door.

Although Dad had gotten Geraldine away from the piano, I wasn't sure what she was going to do next. "Well, I'll see you around," I said, but my mother heard me. "Aren't you going to invite your friend in, Neil?" she asked, and then it was impossible not to.

Joe/Jason was dying to come in and look around anyway; I could tell by the way he accepted the invitation right off and the way his eyes were jumping all around the place like they were electric. I kind of don't know Joe/Jason well enough to figure out if he's really my friend or was just curious to see if Gerri was some kind of freak who would take off her clothes and dance around the carpet in her underwear or do something just as wild that the kids at school would love to hear all about. I just crossed my fingers and prayed that Gerri wouldn't do anything too weird.

"Would you and your friend like a snack?" my mother asked.

At the moment, Gerri was sitting on the floor near the couch and pushing her fingers into the rug. I thought if we just went straight to my room Joe/Jason might not even notice her.

"No thanks, Mom. We'll just go hang around."

But I was dead wrong. We hadn't taken one step when Geraldine spotted us, and one look at Joe/Jason and she let out one of her *ha-hee-hi-heeees*, which rooted Joe/Jason right to the floor. It was sort of a welcoming laugh and in a minute she had scrambled up and was coming right towards him—shuffle/shuffle, shuffle/shuffle. She was learning to put speed on it.

I could see Joe didn't know what to do and so just stood there frozen, not moving, the way people do when a two-thousand-dollar vase is about to topple off a table.

Which gave Geraldine a great opportunity to come over and throw her arms around Joe/Jason and give him a hug like he was her best friend and she hadn't seen him in five years.

Poor Joe/Jason. He let a sort of little laugh come out of his throat and his face turned the color of sunsets and his eyes rolled up in his head.

"That's enough, Geraldine," I said, and she let go. She said, "Dasher-dancer," and let her mouth stay open like she was going to say something else.

"What did she say?" Joe/Jason wanted to know.

"Let's forget it. Let's go to my room," I said.

"Vixen-blix," Gerri said, and Joe/Jason said, "What did she say? Is that how she talks? Can you understand her? How do you know what she's saying? Why is her head banged up?" And then we passed my parents' bedroom and he saw the mess in there and he said, "Hey, you're not moving, are you?"

"Listen," I said, trying not to get annoyed. "Did you come in here to visit or to ask questions?"

"Take it easy," Joe/Jason said. "Don't be sensitive. She's not that bad. Really."

I was glad Joe/Jason wasn't there that night, at dinner. My mother made meatballs and spaghetti because she thought those foods would be soft enough for Gerri to chew, but I guess Gerri didn't like the look of what was on her plate, or maybe it reminded her of something she didn't want to be reminded of. I remembered what Dad had said about trying to get her to eat carrots. She wouldn't touch the spaghetti. My mother begged her and I showed her how to wrap it around a fork and my father said, "C me on, Gerri, dig in," but Gerri just sat at the taole staring at the food and looking as if she was going to burst into tears.

My mother's face was very red, partly from cooking and partly from worry. She said Gerri hadn't eaten anything except oatmeal for breakfast and an ice-cream cone at the park and might get undernourished if she didn't learn to eat solid food.

She put the fork in Gerri's hand and tried to guide it into her mouth, but the spaghetti fell off the fork and some of it fell on the table and some slid into Gerri's lap. I said, "Yuk." My father got up and said he really wasn't that hungry and would just grab a sandwich before he went to bed. A minute later we heard him at the piano and my mother and I had to practically sit on Gerri to keep her from running into the living room after him.

Then I got a really great idea. "I think she's just used to mushy food," I said, and I ran to the cupboard and looked for something soft she might like. I found a jar of applesauce and put it into a dish. Right away Gerri's eyes lit up. I set the dish on the table where she could see it and I said, "Spaghetti first, then applesauce." I pointed to each thing to make it clear that she had to eat some of what she thought was the bad stuff to get the good stuff, and you know, it worked! I'm not saying she didn't make a mess of the spaghetti; the kitchen looked like we'd had a tomato-sauce explosion—but a plate of spaghetti and one meatball went down Gerri's hatch! My mother told me she didn't know what she'd do without me—and now would I please take out the garbage? Some reward!

"Why do I always have to take the garbage out?" I said because that's what I say every night when my mother or father reminds me to do it, and all of a sudden Gerri said, "Bobbidge," very clearly. "Bobbidge." It didn't sound like any of the reindeer; she was trying to say "Garbage"! "Did you hear that, Mom?" I asked, and I could see my mother had heard it all right; she was standing at the sink with the dish rag in her hand smiling from ear to ear.

"She wants to take out the garbage!" I said. "And I'm sure as anything going to teach her!"

At first my mother looked uncertain, but then she said, "I suppose it's safe enough," and she handed me the bag of trash out of the container and said, "Please, be very careful and stay with her every minute, Neil."

So Geraldine and I went down the hall to the incinerator, which is a sort of closet in which there's a little door in the wall that opens like an oven, and you simply throw the bag of garbage through the door and it travels down a chute to the basement. Easy. Geraldine looked really interested. She watched me do it, then I took her back to the apartment and gave her a paper bag and filled it with some junk I pulled out of a wastebasket and I said, "Now you do it, Gerri."

Gerri and I went back to the incinerator together and sure enough, she pushed her own bag of garbage down the incinerator very efficiently, just like she'd been doing it all her life. "Great!" I said. "Good job!" and she looked really thrilled. She said, "Bobbidge, bobbidge!"

I felt great. She loved doing it! From now on, it would be *her* job. I'd never have to take out the bobbidge again!

eight

IT WAS ANOTHER BAD NIGHT. I WOKE UP AT THE INKY hour of 2:24 to the sounds of Gerri's head blamming against my wall. Going back to sleep was out, so I lay awake counting blams, hoping they'd stop of their own accord, and trying to work out ways we could keep a pillow tied around Gerri's head so we could all get a good night's sleep.

Pretty soon I heard my mother's bed creak and then her footsteps heading for Gerri's room.

Then I heard the telephone.

It rang and rang, and finally I heard my father pick up the receiver. I couldn't hear everything he said, but I did hear a lot of "sorrys" and "We're doing our bests."

I heard him tell my mother that it was Mr. Rasmussen from downstairs and that he'd said he'd lived in this building for twenty-two years and in all that time he'd never heard this kind of commotion and if we were going to practice for the Olympics up there, would we do it while he was at work?

Finally I heard my mother rocking Gerri and humming, and pretty soon the place quieted down and I went to sleep thinking how funny it would be if we had to tie a pillow around Mr. Rasmussen's head too.

Being up half the night meant I had to make up for lost sleep sometime; unfortunately, I fell asleep during Miss Lynch's third-period history and was late for old lady Bowring's class, which meant my seat next to Joe/Jason was taken up by Beef Adams, who is called Beef because his arms look like something you'd see hanging in the window of a butcher's shop and he has the brains of a hamburger. I sure was not going to displace Beef, so I had to move into the last available seat, so close to old lady Bowring's desk I could be asphyxiated by her perfume, which smells like an explosion at the florist's.

"Neil, in last night's reading, you learned that the hero of the story 'October Saturday' by Lionel Wycks made a very important catch. Can you tell the class what that catch was?"

Old lady Bowring was probably zeroing in on me because she hadn't seen my face up this close since the beginning of the year. I thought fast, remembering the spear-fishing in Canada assignment I hadn't read, and I crossed my fingers. "Blue mackerel?" I said. I did not say it loud because I wasn't sure it was right, but I said it loud enough for her to hear.

She screwed up her mouth and opened her eyes wide like I'd told her I'd just tied the principal to the flagpole. "Neil Oxley, did you say 'blue mackerel'?" she said in a voice that sounded like it was coming out over the public address system. *"Blue mackerel?"*

The class went wild. It turned out that "October Saturday" was not a story about Canadian spear-fishing, it was a football story and the catch in question was a forward pass, not a fish. Everybody laughed for about ten minutes while I felt the blood rushing up to my head and turning me the color of October leaves, and finally old lady Bowring held up her hand to shut everybody up and ordered me to do not one but two reports, one on last week's spear-fishing story and one on this week's football story and to have them in by tomorrow, *or else*.

As if that wasn't enough, as soon as English period was over, every kid in the class went out of his way to call me blue mackerel at least twice and to stop me in the hall later to ask me what kind of bait to use for a touchdown and did I keep worms in my helmet. Even Joe/Jason, supposed to be my friend, came over to ask me to tell him "about the quarterback that got away."

"Not funny," I said. I was really down now, because it might take me all afternoon and half the night to do those reports, which would hardly leave me time for sleeping, let alone practicing the Franklin Pierce Follies music. I had looked the music over, and what Joe/Jason had called *Plink Plink Plink* was six pieces, long enough to give even Beethoven piano-player's cramp.

Now Joe/Jason broke another piece of bad news. Wendy Wellington had decided to try out for the piano solos too. Wendy Wellington is no older than I am and she hasn't been playing any longer either, but when Wendy Wellington sits down at the piano it sounds like she has twenty-five fingers and an extra ten keys.

"Oh no!" I groaned, when Joe/Jason broke the news.

"Tough break," Joe/Jason said.

It was a bad day for the blue mackerel.

The moment I walked through the door at home, Gerri came from out of nowhere and threw her arms around me and gave me one of her specialty hugs. I took a minute to show her how to shake hands instead of hug and she said, "Blixen blix." It was anybody's guess if she understood what I was trying to tell her.

I didn't stop for a snack or anything, just said hello to my mother and went straight to my bedroom. I had to get going on my reports if I didn't want to be up all night, but right away Gerri was in the doorway, wanting to keep me company and talk reindeer talk to me. "Buzz off," I said. "I'm busy. Go. Can't you see I'm *doing* something?"

"I have to go out for a short while to get some groceries, Neil," my mother called from the kitchen. "Will you keep an eye on Gerri for a half-hour or so?"

What could I say? Mom can't take Gerri to the market without climbing up and down six flights of stairs, and there's no telling what kind of a commotion Gerri would cause hugging the fruit-and-vegetable man, the checkout ladies, and who knows how many customers, so I pulled up a chair and gave Gerri some of my photo albums to look at while I read. She sat in the chair and turned the pages and was very careful not to rip the pictures like I told her, but she kept making sounds and talking—"Dasha, dansa" and so on—making it very hard for me to concentrate on anything, let alone striped bass and halibut, which are not exactly the world's most interesting subjects anyway.

I don't think I'd read more than three pages when my father came home. He was early, and before he'd even taken off his jacket, he was in the doorway of my room asking me why I wasn't practicing for the tryouts. I told him I had this important English assignment to finish first, and he looked just like Gerri had looked when we tried to make her eat spaghetti—like he was being punished. He said he'd come home early to help me work on it since we only had three more days to get it perfect. "Neil, do you think you could work on your English assignment after dinner?" he said.

I couldn't let him down if he'd come home especially to help me. I put aside the reports, and he and I went into the living room and sat down together at the piano and he began to play the first piece through so I'd get an idea of how it should sound. Of course, Gerri came shuffling in right behind us.

My father stopped playing. "Gerri, please go play in your room for a while, honey," he said.

Gerri looked at me; she looked at Dad.

She was working her lips as if she was going to say something, but it was as if her mouth was temporarily out of order; nothing but a little squeak came out. I wouldn't have minded her sitting on the floor listening, but I guess Dad was afraid she was going to try to climb the piano again.

"Go on, Geraldine, go to your room," he said.

Geraldine gave me a sort of sad, good-by look and turned and went step/stepping to her room. After being put away so long I guess Gerri now wanted to be in on everything. Dad said, "I think it'll be easier to concentrate now, don't you, Neil?" and he began to go through the first piece again, pointing out the tricky part right near the end where I'd be playing six complicated chords in a row.

Not a minute later, *FROOM!* A noise that sounded like a mid-air jet collision came from my sister's room and, no kidding, I almost jumped a foot off the piano bench. Dad and I went running, bumping into my mother in the hall. She had just come in and was still holding her bag of groceries and trying to catch her breath.

My sister had done it again—torn down the curtains and curtain rods, like she wanted a better view or—and I couldn't help thinking this—more attention.

Now my father looked really annoyed and he turned to my mother and said, "I think she needs a bit of discipline, don't you?" and my mother nodded her head yes, but didn't answer.

"If we don't get firm, it's going to get out of hand, Margery," my father said.

Gerri was sitting on the edge of her bed with Woodie in her lap. Her mouth was open and the corners were wet. Her eyes looked watery too. With Gerri it was always hard to tell what she was thinking, but I was beginning to be able to tell by the way she held her head and the way her eyebrows moved over her eyes how she was feeling. Now I thought she was feeling scared.

My mother set down the groceries and went over and sat next to her and put her arm around Geraldine's shoulders. "Gerri, please don't do it again," she said, very quietly. Gerri's head turned very slowly on her neck, like there was a battery in it and it was wearing down. She just looked right straight at my mother and her tongue moved in her mouth like she was trying hard to say something but it wouldn't come out.

Then my father made a sound that was half cough and half snort and he said, "Margery, do you call that discipline?'' and he turned, put his hand on my shoulder and headed me back in the direction of the piano.

It was really not easy to concentrate. Although I kept my eye on the music, I kept making mistakes, hitting the wrong key or hitting two keys with one finger, and I had to start the same piece about four times before I could get three bars played without a mistake.

"Ted! Is she in here with you? Where is Gerri? I can't find her!'' My mother came running into the living room. She had a wild look in her eyes. "I just went into the bathroom for two minutes and when I came out, she'd disappeared.''

"She must be in the apartment,'' my father said, jumping up from the piano bench. My father had put special locks on the windows so we knew she could never get out that way. Still, my parents looked worried, so I checked out all the closets and looked under the beds. There was no sign of Gerri anywhere in the apartment.

Dad found her out in the hall a few minutes later. It was funny, but not really funny.

She'd gone to empty the "bobbidge'' all by herself, just the way I'd shown her. Only instead of the trash, she'd thrown my mother's unpacked bag of groceries down the chute.

How would I explain to old lady Bowring tomorrow that now I had to run down to the supermarket to buy the stuff that Gerri had thrown away while my mother started dinner and my father worked on trying to put back the rods in Gerri's room? How would I tell her that after dinner I'd have to help my mother clean up the mess Gerri would make with the pot roast and mashed potatoes and that I'd then fall asleep right in the middle of "October Saturday" before I'd written one word of the report? How would I explain that although I'd set my alarm to wake me an hour early in the morning, the midnight head-blamming kept me up for so long that I not only slept through the alarm but almost missed the school bus?

I couldn't tell her. Which is why fourth-period Wednesday turned into Black Sunday, and sent me to the principal's office for the first time in my life.

nine

I PRACTICALLY HAD TO PINCH MYSELF TO STAY AWAKE during third period. Miss Lynch was discussing the Continental Congress, and if she hadn't shown some gory slides of the battle scenes of the Revolutionary War, I would have been off to dreamland. Which is the last thing I wanted, since I absolutely had to be in Bowring's class early if I wanted even a fighting chance to get a back seat.

I figured if I got a back seat today, Mrs. Bowring was sure to forget the assignment she'd given me and I'd have another day to get it done before the hatchet fell. On the other hand, if I had to sit anywhere in her three-row radar range, she'd remember the two reports and it would mean the frying pan for the blue mackerel.

I really flew from Miss Lynch's class on the second floor to old lady Bowring's on the first. My feet hardly touched the ground. Sure enough—and what a relief!—I was one of the first kids in class and there were lots of seats left in the last few rows. I slid into my usual seat next to Joe/Jason, who was already in his, studying the script for his part in the Franklin Pierce Follies. The actors had tried out last week and as usual, Joe/Jason got one of the leads: he was going to play Franklin Pierce and already had the home-economics bunch sewing him a custom-made sheet for the scene where he appears as Pierce's ghost. Everyone liked Joe/Jason, especially Joe/Jason. "How does this sound?" he said to me and read the first line: "I've come back from the dead. What's new in town?"

"Great," I said. "Sounds great."

"Should I put more emphasis on 'new' or 'town'?" he said, re-reading his script. I was more interested in keeping an eye on the door to see if maybe I was going to get a real shot of luck; could Bowring please be absent just for this once in my lifetime?

Not a chance. She probably hadn't been absent since Franklin Pierce was President and they built, not this school, but the school that used to be here before this one. Sure enough, with books under each arm, in she came, glasses, white hair, flowered dress and all, and plumped all her stuff on her desk, ready for action.

At which time, Beef Adams, hair flying, shirt flying, face the color of a slice of bologna, came into class just as the bell was about to ring. He made his way to the back of the classroom, although it was clear as glass to me that the only seats left were the ones in the front, and believe it or not, he was heading right in my direction. Actually, he wasn't only heading right in my direction, he was heading for my seat, although it was obvious that someone was in it. Me.

He planted his big beefy self smack in front of me and had the nerve to say, "This is my seat, so swim off, blue mackerel."

Old lady Bowring was checking through the attendance book and couldn't see back this far anyway, so she wasn't aware of what Beef was doing.

"What do you mean, *your* seat?"

"My seat," Beef said, and he pointed at the desk. There, carved fresh into the wood, were his initials—B.A.

While I'd been wasting my time drawing flags of the world in my notebook, he'd been monogramming school desks.

"Get up, Fish," he said again.

Now Joe/Jason leaned over and said to Beef, "Leave Neil alone, willya? You can see he was here before you."

Now here's what I mean about Franklin Pierce Junior High School. Beef Adams was dead wrong, anybody could see that, and I was dead right, as any fair jury would admit. But Beef is an East-Ender and old lady Bowring's class was full of other East-Enders. Right away, they overruled Joe/Jason and turned against me.

"Come on, Mackerel, Beef hasn't done his homework, give him a break," one of them whispered.

Another one said, "Go swim upstream, willya, Mack?"

And another one said, "Let's get a net and pull him out of his chair!"

While Beef had his group pulling for him, all I had was Joe/Jason, and it was no contest. With everybody cheering for Beef, he got a big surge of self-confidence and he leaned over and tried to lift me out of the chair with his big steaks-and-chops arms. I wouldn't budge. He pulled, I resisted. While Joe/Jason said, "Come on, Beef, lay off," in one trying-hard but single voice, four other guys and one girl were in there for Beef.

"WHAT . . . IS . . . GOING. . . ON . . . BACK . . . THERE?"

Good, grey grief! Had old lady Bowring had her eyeglass prescription changed? How come she'd noticed us back here anyway? Her voice ricocheted around the room like they'd emptied a cage of parakeets in here. Now she was headed this way!

Even with Bowring coming at us through the aisle a mile a minute, Beef didn't stop. He had me by the shirt and was trying to pull me up. I was holding on to the desk with both hands. He had his cheering section and I had my Joe/Jason and it made quite a commotion: a lot of furniture seemed to be shaking, and under my feet, the floor didn't seem all that steady, either.

"WHAT . . . IS . . . HAPPENING . . . HERE?"

Beef let go. I let go. Everybody shut up, one-two-three.

Bowring grabbed my shoulder and Beef's arm. Was she trying to perfume us to death? She squinted at us through her glasses.

"Come to the desk, both of you," she ordered. I expected fire to come out of her nose and mouth, or at least smoke. That's how mad she sounded.

I followed Beef up to her desk. He followed her. She asked what was going on back there. I mumbled, "Nothing," and Beef mumbled, "Nothing." She did not look happy with two nothings. She asked for Beef's assignment. Beef hadn't done it. She asked for my assignment. I hadn't done it. She turned blue. Well, not exactly, but she looked like she might.

She told us to get our books and to go sit in Mr. Guttag's office. She said she would have no fighting in her classroom. She said no one would accuse her of being permissive and encouraging wanton behavior. Nobody knew what "wanton" meant but we knew it wasn't good. She said she knew times were changing but they weren't going to change in *her* classroom. I wished like anything times would change and that it would be July or August when schools were closed. Instead, here were Beef and I, making our way to Mr. Guttag's office.

"Sit down, boys," said Mr. Guttag's secretary, who hardly looked up from her typewriter. "Mr.

Guttag is in his private office now. He'll see you in a few minutes."

While we waited I tried to listen for screams to see if somebody else was really getting it in there, but the typewriter was making so much noise there was no telling. Besides, my stomach felt like high tide and I had to concentrate on keeping it under control. Beef just sat next to me relaxed as anything, humming (humming!) like he was sitting here waiting for the light to change, like he did this every day.

But Mr. Guttag did not seem to recognize Beef. He just stepped out of his office and strode over to us in three or four big steps and stood looking down at us as if he were trying to decide whether to throw us into a reptile pit or simply tie us to these chairs and beat us with chains for a couple of hours.

"Boys," he said. He made the word "boys" sound like the Gettysburg Address spoken by Lincoln to a million people. Even the secretary stopped typing to listen.

"Boys, Mrs. Bowring just called me on the intercom to tell me that you caused a disturbance in class."

Mr. Guttag made "disturbance" sound like "holocaust." Then he paused. "She said that there was a . . . scuffle. Is that correct?" He made "scuffle" sound like "earthquake."

I nodded. Beef had stopped humming. He nodded.

"Boys. I want you to understand that we are not going to tolerate this sort of behavior in our school. I am putting this to you in the form of a warning, since this is a first offense. Let me make it clear by putting it to you this way: I expect you to behave at all times like gentlemen. Is that understood?"

I nodded. Beef nodded.

"In short," said Mr. Guttag, "I do not want to see you in this office again."

Right. I was for that, one hundred percent. I didn't want to be in Mr. Guttag's office ever again, either. Beef nodded. I nodded. Mr. Guttag shook my hand, then he shook Beef's hand. I was so relieved, I felt like doing a dance right outside the office in the corridor. No snakes! No chains! We were free!

"Don't worry," I wanted to say, "you'll never see me in this office again, Mr. Guttag!" But I was wrong.

I didn't know it then, but I was going to be back very soon—and the next time was going to be a lot worse.

ten

THERE WAS NO FOOLING AROUND THIS TIME. I CAME
home, went right to my room, closed the door, and
got to work on my English reports. With the house
this quiet, I could practically zip through the work,
so by the time my mother and Gerri got home,
from wherever they'd gone, I'd finished one report
and gotten halfway through the other. My mother
was in a very good mood. She said she'd found a
school that would take Gerri for a few hours every
day and teach her letters and numbers. My mother
was sure Gerri could be taught to read first-grade
words.

Gerri did seem to love turning the pages of
books. She couldn't seem to get enough of my photograph albums. I had pictures of all my friends at
the old school pasted in there, and some very good
shots I'd taken at Lake Alfred, where we always
rent a summer cottage. I took a picture of a deer

that could have won a contest (except part of his tail was cut off by the camera) and a picture of my mother and father sitting in a rowboat before my father grew his moustache.

Gerri was full of "donder and blitzens"; she was talking a mile a minute as she was turning the pages of my albums; I thought I ought to tell my mother to buy Gerri a scrapbook and some scissors and get her started with a hobby that would take her mind off pulling down curtains. Gerri was being so quiet in my room I actually got to finish my second report and no kidding, it turned out better than my first. I stuck it into my ring-binder notebook and felt pretty pleased with myself. I might even go sit in the first row of old lady Bowring's class tomorrow to give her a break and knock all the kids off their chairs with surprise.

I was in a great mood. My reports were done, I could smell chicken frying, and I'd even have time to work on my Follies piano piece after dinner. I looked over at Gerri sitting in my rocker and it was like Joe/Jason had said: she wasn't that bad. Once she stopped banging her head and the black-and-blue bumps went down, she would look fine. In the meantime, she was calming down and I didn't mind her hugging me all the time. She wasn't a spoiled brat like other sisters I knew either; you could give her any little thing, like a blue cake of soap or something, and she'd just act like it was Christmas. And no kidding, even if she laughed in the wrong places sometimes, I think she understood a lot of what was going on. Like teasing. She was terrific to tease. If I threw Woodie up in the air she screamed like she was being attacked by the vampire bats, but then—here's the best part—she'd never even try to tell on me. I was tattle-proof.

When Dad got home, I could tell right away he was in a good mood too. He said on the way home he'd gotten an inspiration for a new song he was going to call "You Put a Firecracker in My Heart" and right after he helped me with my Follies piece, he was going to get to work on it.

Dinner went well too: we had the applesauce routine down pat—Gerri knew she'd get some in a dish if she ate some food she had to chew, and to-night she almost looked as if she liked the drum-stick my mother gave her. She smiled and laughed a lot of *ha hi hees* and my father looked really pleased.

After dinner, my mother said she had to put up her aching feet for a few minutes, and she went into the bedroom to lie down and watch TV. Dad and I cleared the table and loaded the dishwasher and Gerri took out the garbage (I watched very carefully to make sure that only garbage went), and I also tried to teach her to sweep, which she loved. Unfortunately, she took forever to get the crumbs into the dustpan, and as soon as she'd gotten them all swept up she'd pour them out on the floor again so she could start all over.

As soon as Dad and I had the kitchen spic-and-span, we sent Gerri in to watch TV with my mother and headed right for the piano.

Dad thought I should warm up by playing some scales first, so I played the C and G scales and some chords, and Dad gave me some pointers about how to hold my wrists down. Then I tried to run through the second Follies piece and it was harder than the first—written in the key of B flat and very tricky in the chorus. "It needs a little work, but don't worry, you'll do fine," Dad said, but I was worried. Tryouts were the day after tomorrow, I was up against Wendy Wellington, and I hadn't even had the time to go through all the pieces once.

Dad saw my face and gave me a little lecture on trying hard, perseverance, staying power, and never quitting. He told me how his father had forced him to play for two hours every day and how he'd hated Grandpa for it at the time but was now very grateful and wished he could write a letter to Grandpa in heaven to tell him. I pointed out that I only had two days to practice and it looked pretty hopeless, and Dad said that there was no such word as hopeless in his vocabulary. He said we had the whole evening before us and now, the apartment being peaceful and quiet, there was no excuse for not diving right into the piece and working it through until I had it down pat and perfect, and to please note that it said *"Vivace,"* which meant brisk and lively.

I began to play briskly and lively, and couldn't

have played more than six bars when we heard my mother scream. It wasn't a regular "Dracula's attacking!" scream, it was more the sort of "Oh, no" cry, like in an opera when the soprano discovers that her boyfriend has been stabbed through the heart by a clown. It had come from the kitchen.

My father jumped up. I jumped up. I saw my father's teeth for a second under his moustache and I heard him say, "Damn," which I think he didn't want me to hear him say. He also said, "Margery, what's happened now?"

I couldn't believe the kitchen scene. Every can of food and soup was out of the cupboard, lined up all over the place. My mother was standing at the stove, both hands clapped over her mouth. Gerri was backed up against the refrigerator. She'd taken about three-quarters of the labels off the cans, and left what looked like a million plain tin cans standing in unidentifiable, identical bunches on the table, chairs, and floor.

"I was watching television and must have fallen asleep," my mother said. My mother was talking through her hands, which still were covering her mouth and made it hard to understand her.

My father's eyebrows moved towards each other. "Geraldine! What the hell did you do that for?" he cried.

Geraldine burst into tears. She cries funny, in very loud, crazy gasps. She started crying and gasping and all of a sudden turned her head toward the refrigerator. Oh, no! She wasn't going to do the head bit now? Sure enough, she began thwacking her head against the Westinghouse and the racket was terrible. My mother rushed over and put her arms around her. "Gerri, Gerri, please, please! It's all right, darling, it's all right!"

The telephone began to ring.

My father shook his head. "Oh, Margery," he groaned, and he kept rubbing his moustache and shaking his head. Then he said, "I'm sorry," but I don't think my mother heard him. The thwacking noise was awful.

My father pretended the telephone wasn't ringing; he just ignored it. He put his arm around me and he said, "Come on, Neil, let's go out for a walk," and he and I left my mother and my sister and we walked out of the apartment.

I was really worried about leaving my mother alone there with Gerri; I knew the telephone call was coming from Mr. Rasmussen or someone else who was really mad. What would he do if no one answered? Would he call the police or come upstairs himself and try to push his way into the apartment? My father told me not to worry. He said the door was locked, my mother was safe, and he wanted to get me out of the house for a walk and a private little talk.

On Sundays we sometimes go to a little park near our building, but at night the park isn't safe, so my father and I walked eight blocks to a new ice-cream place on Albermarle Avenue, even though it was drizzling and we hadn't taken an umbrella.

All the time we were walking, he didn't say much. When we got to the ice-cream place he looked up at the sign listing the twenty-five flavors and he said, "I can't make up my mind. What would you like, Neil?" and I said I wanted pistachio mint, a double dip, so my father ordered that for me and he ordered a single cone of butter pecan for himself, but when it came, he just took one lick and said he really wasn't in the mood for ice cream and he threw the whole cone away!

I guess he wasn't in the mood for talking much either, because all he said was that he thought I wasn't practicing enough piano, and that he wasn't practicing much either. Then he just stood there looking around and waiting for me to finish my cone, like he was more in the mood for thinking than talking.

On the way home, he hardly spoke at all until we were on the corner of Albermarle and Third, waiting for the light to change. Then he suddenly asked me if I'd be happier if we sent Gerri back to the Training Center.

The question really surprised me. Had Dad really thought of doing that, no kidding? I couldn't imagine Dad packing Gerri into the ord and taking her back to the school, dumping her off back there with her suitcase, and leaving her there for good.

I didn't want to tell him that sometimes she

reminded me of me, and that a lot of times I thought that what happened to her could have happened to me if I'd been born first.

"What do you say, Neil?" my father said. He was looking up at the sky like someone up there was going to throw down an envelope with the answer in it.

"I don't think so. She doesn't bother me that much," I said, and I know he heard me, but he didn't answer, and all the rest of the way home, he didn't say a word.

When we got back to the apartment, everything had quieted down. Gerri was in her room (I could hear her talking to Woodie) and my mother was putting away the last of the unlabeled cans.

"We brought home some ice cream," my father said, and my mother put it into the freezer.

"We're going to be glad to have good desserts, because something tells me with all these unmarked cans we're going to be eating some really funny meals," my mother said. She tried to smile, but only the right side of her mouth seemed to want to go up.

"Why do you suppose Gerri wanted to take all those labels off the cans?" I asked her.

"I don't know, but I bet she had a perfectly logical reason," my mother said.

I didn't really believe my mother then, but I found out Gerri's logical reason the very next day, and I think it took about ten years off my life.

eleven

IT HAD BEEN ANOTHER BAD NIGHT. HEAD-BANGING, the telephone, and something new: another neighbor pounded on our living room wall with what sounded like lead boxing gloves—probably Mr. and Mrs. Rawlings, who had a new baby and lived next door in 6-D.

Pretty soon we would have to either get pillows for everyone on the floor to tie around their heads or furnish Gerri's room with sandbags. While I was lying there, trying to get myself back to sleep, listening to my mother rocking Gerri, I heard my father's voice in the bedroom. He said a bad word. I heard it. Then I heard *CRACK*, and I wasn't sure what had made that sound until later, when I heard it again. It was my father's fist, hitting the wall.

When my alarm rang, I didn't hear it. I slept right through, as if it were Saturday. When I did wake up, it was so late I had no time for breakfast and hardly enough time to brush my teeth or comb my hair.

Then I couldn't find my ring-binder notebook. I flew around the apartment like my shoes were on fire; my English reports were in there, both of them! I couldn't show up in Bowring's class without the reports today!

My mother is the best looker-for-lost-things— she always finds whatever is missing. This time, though, it was Dad who found it. It was hidden in the piano bench, of all places, and of course, we all knew who'd put it in there. Late as I was, I took a minute to run into Gerri's room to scream my head off at her. She just pulled the covers over her head and pretended she didn't hear me.

In the elevator, I met Mr. Rasmussen, who had his Scottie on a blue leash. "What's going on in your apartment?" he said to me. "What are you people doing in there?" He looked angry. He also looked tired.

I didn't know what to say. It's very hard for me to tell people about Gerri. I just looked down at the dog and I didn't answer.

"You people are making such a racket the whole building's up in arms about it," Mr. Rasmussen said. "Something's going to have to be done," he said.

"Yes sir," I said, and I was really relieved when the elevator stopped in the lobby and I ran out.

I was in plenty of time for Bowring's class, in a seat that wasn't in the back but wasn't really up front either. I still had about two minutes before the period started and Bowring arrived, and although Joe/Jason was calling me to come in back and tell him how the practicing was coming and sit next to him and listen to how he'd memorized some more lines, I decided to look over my report one more time before handing it in.

I opened my notebook, looked at my report, and good, grey grief, I think all the blood ran out of my head. No kidding, I expected to see a red puddle right at my feet on the floor. My report—all that careful work about Canadian spear-fishing and Saturday football that took me forever to put together, which I copied in my best handwriting, which I'd put in the gorgeous blue folder and lettered ENGLISH REPORT in the most careful, indelible-ink letters, measured with a ruler—was covered with the labels from our canned goods!

Gerri! While Dad and I were out having ice cream last night, she must have been busy making a scrapbook by sticking in paper labels that read Tuna, Ravioli, Beets, and Mandarin Orange Sections!

I guess she'd gotten the idea from seeing me paste stuff in my photo album, borrowed my glue and wrecked my report!

In a minute, Bowring would be in here, asking for it, opening the blue cover, seeing the Campbell Split Pea Soup label, the Kernel Corn label, the

Green Pea label with the Jolly Green Giant on it. If she looked up and said to me in front of the class, "What is the meaning of this, Neil? Why did you paste green-pea labels in your report?" and if she then held it up for the class to see, turned the pages, squinted at them through her glasses while the class rolled on the floor laughing, it would feel like Gerri had torn *me* up into little bits.

I couldn't face it. I had only one minute to run, and I jumped up, grabbed the book, and, no kidding, I ran. I flew out of Bowring's class like someone had flung me out the door like a frisbee. I whooshed through the halls and, not knowing where to go, ducked into the boys' room just as the bell rang. She hadn't seen me. I was safe.

A few East-Enders were in there passing around a cigarette. One of them was from English class, Dick Franzella, who, it was said, only attended classes on Franklin Pierce's birthday. "You cutting Bowring too?" he asked me, and offered me a drag. I didn't like the smell of the cigarette so I shook my head.

"Yeah, I'm cutting Bowring too," I said.

"Join the club," he said.

To tell the truth, this was the first time I'd ever cut a class, and I felt like I felt the first time I'd been out on my uncle's sailboat on Lake Alfred—like I was going to tip over, maybe drown. Any minute I expected the door of the boys' room to open and a teacher to burst in and line us up against the tile wall and ask each one his name and why he wasn't in class. A few times the door slid open, but it was only some kid or other wanting to go to the bathroom, but each time it was like my heart left my body and just hung in the air waiting to get back in my chest and start beating again. The other guys were just sitting around smoking and rapping and telling dirty jokes; they were used to this and looked like they were having fun.

I just stood around waiting for the period to end; half the time I just sat in one of the cubicles so that if a teacher did come in I wouldn't be caught.

Finally, after what seemed like a longer time than an all-night hike, the period ended. When the bell rang I walked out in the hall and pretended to act normal, although any minute I expected old lady Bowring to pop out in front of me, grab me by the T-shirt, and drag me off to Mr. Guttag's office.

Which never happened at all. I stayed pretty much out of sight, steered clear of the cafeteria, the library, and the central corridor, and it turned out not to be a bad day at all—until last period. I was at my locker getting my jacket when Beef Adams came up.

He made a fist and punched me in the shoulder, which is his idea of a friendly greeting. "Whaddya say, Neil," he said, very friendly.

"Hi," I said. I was kind of surprised, since I never get any attention from Beef unless it's a putdown or an argument. I was alert.

"You cut Bowring, huh?" he said. It was like a

compliment. His eyes were shining with new respect.

"Yeah," I said, trying to sound casual. Even the word "cut" makes me think of swords and knives and gives me the jitters. Had anyone heard?

"How come?" Beef asked. No one else was around, but I didn't want to talk about my cutting at all, least of all to Beef.

"She knows you cut, y'know," Beef said. He said it really casual, like he was telling me what size shoes he wears or that it's going to rain.

"She knows?" My own voice went right up, like I was trying out for the seventh-grade choir. "How does she know?"

"When she took attendance, some helpful kid, I think it was Sally Brown-noser Gibbons, yelled out, 'He's here; I just saw him,' and somebody else chimed in 'yeah, he's here all right,' like that. Only you weren't."

My heart moved right out of my body again. I just stared at Beef. Of course, I knew I'd be caught. Everybody who cuts gets caught sooner or later (even the bunch in the bathroom, who love being suspended). Still, I thought that maybe I'd get away with it this once.

"Listen, it ain't that bad for a first offender," Beef offered. "Guttag just hangs you by your thumbs for a couple of days, first time around, haha." Beef was practically doubling over at his own joke.

"Problem is, it's not exactly first time around," I said in my own crazy new voice, having to remind him we'd just done a little time in Guttag's office yesterday.

Beef looked thoughtful. "Oh yeah," he said. Then his face brightened. "Don't worry, Neil. I can fix it for you," he said.

"You can?" I said. "How?"

"I've done it a hundred times. I got a friend, works in the guidance counselor's office during his free period. When the cut slips come in, he makes yours disappear, that's all. That way they never get to Guttag's office, and they never get sent home, either."

"No kidding." In spite of myself, I was feeling as if someone had given me a little bouquet of hope.

"Only thing is, I got to give my friend two dollars."

Leave it to Beef to try to make a little money on other people's misfortunes. He was probably going to keep one dollar himself. Maybe both.

I then remembered I didn't have two dollars. "I only have one dollar," I said. If I'd gone to the cafeteria and eaten lunch today, I wouldn't even have had that.

"Okay, just this once, as a special favor to me, maybe he'll do it for only one dollar," Beef said, and he snapped the money right out of my hand the minute I took it out of my pocket.

"Are you sure you can take care of it?" I asked.

"Good as done, Neil, rest your mind and keep cool," he said, and he tucked the dollar into his wallet and pushed the wallet into his back pocket.

"Thanks, Beef," I said, and the truth is, I felt much better. Dummy that I am, I actually trusted him.

twelve

AT HOME, AFTER MY MOTHER STOPPED ME FROM threatening my sister with one of my old galoshes to illustrate what I was going to do to her if she ever touched my school stuff again, I tried to peel the food labels off my report and maybe salvage some of it, but the pages tore, so I had to start working from scratch. This time nothing short of an invasion from Mars would stop me from finishing the report and handing it in to Mrs. Bowring tomorrow.

If there was time I'd practice the piano tonight, and if there wasn't, I'd have to get up at five in the morning and practice then. If I didn't, I wouldn't have a chance of being in the Follies. I'd go through the rest of my school days alone—the weird kid without a group, wandering around the place like the man without a country.

My mother was in Gerri's room, trying to teach

her how to tie shoelaces. When I calmed down I told her three times I couldn't be disturbed. Despite the galoshes, Gerri gave me a big smile and a shriek. Her head bumps looked bluer than ever and I noticed that the curtains were down again. My mother said she understood I needed privacy and quiet for studying, and speaking of studying, how was school today?

I started to tell her about cutting English, but at the last minute I changed my mind. My mother was getting those circles under the eyes that old people get and she was hardly smiling any more. I told her school was fine. She told me Gerri would not be starting her school until autumn, which seemed a long way off.

She suggested I go into the kitchen for milk and cookies. She'd wanted to surprise me by baking some with Gerri's help, but when she tried to teach Gerri to break an egg into the batter, Gerri threw the shell in too. In the end my mother had to throw out the batter and go to the store for the cookies. Never mind, I told her, they tasted fine.

I think I cheered her up; a few minutes later she came into the kitchen to show me some pictures she'd taken of Gerri in the park with a Polaroid camera, and she was smiling. One of the pictures, where Gerri's head was turned good side to the camera, came out pretty nice. My mother had bought a really neat frame for it that looked like real white leather, and she said she was going to put it on top of the piano next to the photos of me and Grandpa. Just as she was about to go into the living room with the picture, the telephone rang.

My mother took the receiver off the hook, and although all she said was "Hello," right away I could tell something was wrong. She was standing there with the telephone in one hand and the picture of Gerri in the other and no kidding, her face turned practically the same color as the picture frame.

Usually, when my mother talks on the telephone, she talks. I mean she talks and talks and laughs and talks. This time, she just held the receiver up to her ear and nodded and said, "Yes," a couple of times, and finally, she put the receiver back in its cradle and she just stood there looking at me.

I stopped eating and said, "What's the matter?" and she pretended that everything was fine and said, "Oh, nothing. You want some more cookies?" and I said, "Who was that on the phone?" and then my mother just sank into the chair opposite my chair at the kitchen table and she shook her head and looked down at the place mat like she'd never seen it before.

"It was Mr. Parrish."

Mr. Parrish is the superintendent-manager of the building we live in. He's in charge of everything that goes on—sort of like the big boss of everyone who lives here. He's also pretty tough; I once saw him hold two kids he thought were trying to open the coin boxes in the laundry room until the police came. You don't fool around with Mr. Parrish.

"What did he want?"

"He wants to come up and talk to your father and me tonight," my mother said. She was drawing on the place mat with her finger.

"What for?" I said, but I didn't have to ask. Mr. Parrish was coming up to talk to my parents about Gerri. "Are you letting him come up?" I asked, when my mother didn't answer.

"What else can I do?" she asked.

My father ran to the piano the minute he came home. He said he had an inspiration for the release of "Firecracker" and wanted to get it on paper before it disappeared out of his head. He reached into the piano bench for blank sheet music and began to play chords with his left hand and write with his right. I was sitting on the couch listening and my mother was giving Gerri a bath. Dad suddenly stopped. "Hey, what's this?" he said, spotting Gerri's picture on the piano.

"Mom took it at the park," I said. "It's pretty good, isn't it?"

"It certainly is," Dad said, putting it back between my picture and the picture of Grandpa. "Not bad at all." He went back to playing chords and writing them down.

My mother had heard the music and suddenly

appeared with Gerri. Gerri was in her nightgown and robe and, as usual, had to be held back from trying to climb on the piano.

Dad was in a pretty good mood. "Hi, Gerri! How's my photogenic girl?" he said. He hit a great big beautiful chord, and Gerri let out a squeal. Suddenly, she said, "Gee! Gee! Gee!"

My father stopped playing to look at her.

"It's the key of G," my father said. He played it one more time, never taking his eyes off her.

"Gee!" Gerri yelled.

My father looked really excited. He turned to my mother and lifted his eyebrows.

"Try a different chord," my mother said. She was holding Gerri's towel and squeezing it in her hands.

My father tried another chord.

Gerri squealed, "Gee! Gee! Geee!" again.

My father's face fell. "That wasn't a G chord. It was E sharp," he said. "For a minute there, I thought—"

He stopped talking and played an arpeggio, using both hands and what looked like his elbows and shoulders too. He didn't look at my mother, or at me, or at Gerri.

"You thought she might have perfect pitch too?" my mother asked, over the sound of the music. She was still in the doorway and still hanging like anything on to that wet towel.

"It was kind of a silly idea," my father said. He

kept playing, but his moustache looked like it was drooping.

"It's not a silly idea," my mother said.

"In any case, she doesn't and it doesn't matter," my father said.

Dinner that night was really crazy. With all those unlabeled cans, we were eating really weird combinations. My mother wanted to open a can of kernel corn and got breakfast figs instead. My father ate the breakfast figs with his lamb chop and asked my mother if he was going to have spaghetti and meatballs for breakfast tomorrow. The spinach turned out to be cranberry sauce. My mother made one more attempt at getting a vegetable on the table and let me pick a can. What we hoped was a can of asparagus stalks turned out to be chicken chow mein. For dessert, instead of pineapple, my mother opened a can of pea soup.

My father got up from the table. "I'm not that hungry," he said. "I had a big lunch."

"Let me give you coffee, at least," my mother said, and was getting up when the doorbell rang.

"Who could that be?" asked my father.

My mother looked at me. She hadn't told my father about Mr. Parrish. I suppose she didn't want to upset him and was waiting until after dinner to tell him, like she did the time my ten-speed bicycle was stolen and she wanted to break the news gently, on his full stomach.

"It's Mr. Parrish," she said, looking whiter than ever.

"Mr. Parrish?" my father said and his face looked as if he'd opened the hall closet and the seven dwarfs had jumped out.

"Neil, would you keep Gerri in here while Dad and I go into the living room and talk to him?" My mother looked nervous, the way she looks when anyone runs a high temperature or goes out too far in the ocean at the beach.

I said I'd try. My father got up and said, "What does he want?" but I could tell he already knew pretty well why Mr. Parrish had come up here. He scraped his chair on the floor when he pushed it away from the table like he always tells me not to do, and he and my mother went into the living room.

I really wanted to hear what Mr. Parrish had to say, so I stood at the door trying to listen, but Gerri kept up her steady stream of conversation, and what with all the prancers and dancers coming out of her mouth, I couldn't catch much of what was going on in the living room.

I kept saying, "Shh, Gerri! Shh!" but she just went right on making enough racket to block out any other voices. Which gave me the idea of filling her mouth with food. If she was eating, she'd have to shut up, wouldn't she?

Where was the applesauce? There didn't seem to be any in the refrigerator. I looked into the cupboard, but aside from the rows of unmarked cans and some that still had labels that Gerri had missed, I didn't see anything that would appeal to her. Except, maybe those marshmallows on the top shelf? I thought I saw my mother give her one a couple of days ago. What were they doing all the way up there, anyway? Maybe Gerri liked them so much that Mom had had to put them out of reach?

"Want a marshmallow, Gerri?"

"Pransssssa, blix."

I was beginning to understand her, no kidding. I dragged the step stool over to the cupboard and climbed up two steps and reached in the cupboard for the marshmallows, and while my back was turned and I was up on the ladder, would you believe it? Gerri just got up and started heading for the kitchen door.

"Hey, Gerri! Come back! I'm getting those marshmallows down for you!" I called, but she didn't stop. She'd heard that strange voice in the living room and was heading his way, revving up her shuffle/shuffle to full-speed-ahead to make sure I didn't catch her.

I got off the ladder as fast as I could and ran right out of the kitchen after her, but she was already crossing the living room and heading straight for Mr. Parrish, zeroing right in on him like she had a mission to push him out of the way of a falling building. His back was to Gerri so he didn't see her, but now I could hear what he was saying.

He was saying that he'd had to bring action

against a man who had had all-night marijuana parties in his apartment and he'd had to bring action against a family that was raising rabbits in the master bedroom, but he hoped he wouldn't have to bring action against us. I knew that "bring action" meant turning us out of our apartment, which is the apartment we've lived in ever since I was born.

My father's eyebrows moved together over his eyes, and he said that he wasn't having wild parties or raising rabbits and that Gerri needed time to adjust and why couldn't people be a little patient?

Mr. Parrish was about to answer when he sensed or heard Gerri's footsteps coming his way and he turned around and just stared at her. She was heading directly at him and his expression was like—no kidding—he'd come face to face with twenty kids trying to vandalize the basement washing machines. His mouth went straight across like he was preparing to put a knife between his lips and his body seemed frozen to the corner of the rug, like he was not a person at all, but a wood carving decorating the room.

Gerri never hesitated for a moment. I guess she knew all along why she was headed for Mr. Parrish. She shuffled right up to him, said, "Vixen, vix, blix," and threw her arms around him in a great big bear hug.

For a second, Mr. Parrish looked like he didn't know what hit him. When she let go of him, his mouth looked even straighter, his eyes rounder. There was a second or two of absolute what-next silence and then—no kidding—Mr. Parrish grabbed Geraldine and hugged her right back!

I guess none of us expected that. In fact, all of a sudden, my mother turned her back on all of us; I guess she didn't want us to see her face when she wiped her eyes with the back of her hand. I guess that's the way my mother celebrates! It certainly seemed as if Mr. Parrish really liked Gerri, and if Mr. Parrish liked Gerri, he wouldn't bring action, would he? Even my father's moustache looked as if it was smiling.

I felt good too. I'd finished my reports and hidden my ring-binder out of sight. Beef would fix the cut slip, I still had hours to practice my Follies piece for tomorrow's tryouts, and now it seemed that we could stay right on in our apartment.

Things were looking up. I was sure everything would be smooth and sweet as those marshmallows in the kitchen cupboard and we'd all live happily ever after.

I should have remembered things always look brightest before the storm; no kidding, I'd never been so wrong about the future in my whole life!

thirteen

My father and I decided if I got the first follies piece absolutely perfect I'd have at least an
even chance of getting the piano part, in spite of
Wendy Wellington. There was always the possibility that Wendy wouldn't show up, or that she'd
sprain a finger playing ball since she is also on the
baseball team, or that just for once she'd hit all the
wrong keys and I'd hit the right ones.

My father put aside his firecracker song to help
me practice this one piece, which was called, "Mrs.
Pierce, You Have a Lovely Baby Boy," when my
mother came in to tell us that she hated to disturb
the practicing but that she couldn't get Gerri to
sleep until I stopped playing; the music was keeping her wide awake and making her very excited. I
said okay and closed the piano. I felt I had the
piece down pretty good except for one really tough
part with a lot of sharps and flats in the left hand,

and I was getting pretty tired anyway. My father got up and walked around the room and said that it definitely needed more work.

I told him I'd planned to set the alarm to go off early tomorrow morning to get in some more practicing before tryouts, and he agreed that that was a good idea. As for his own song, he told me he'd met a man who lives on Lafayette Avenue who said he'd let him use his piano now and then, and he was going over there now to work on the release so he wouldn't disturb anyone here.

He took his music out of the piano bench, went in to kiss my mother good-by, and told me to go easy on the right pedal. He wished me luck at the tryouts and he left.

In the middle of the night I heard Gerri's head whamming and blamming, although my mother had moved her bed way out in the middle of her room, hoping that getting her away from a wall would help. I guess Gerri just climbed out of bed and found a wall to use anyway, but I must have been getting used to it; it didn't keep me awake that long, just long enough to hear my father come home and take the phone off the hook when it started to ring.

When the alarm went off at quarter to five, I didn't much feel like getting out of bed, let alone practicing piano. My body felt like somebody had tied a couple of weights to it, and I yawned about fifty times.

I guess I'm not at my best at that hour in the

morning because when the piece was supposed to go *plink, plong, plang,* rest, *plinkity plong,* I kept hitting the wrong key and it came out sounding like *plink, plunk, flam,* rest, *plinkity, flam, flam.* I must have played it seventy times and every time it started right and ended wrong.

All of a sudden, mixed with the plinks and the plunks, I thought I heard a *bling-blang,* but I kept playing. I heard it again: *bling* and *blang.* The doorbell! The doorbell at five in the morning? Following the *blings* and *blangs* came a *whang* and a *bam-bam-bam*; no kidding, it sounded like a gorilla was out in the hall trying to knock our door down with his feet.

I was really scared, although the chain was still on and both locks were locked. I got up from the piano bench and went to the door. "Who is it?" I asked. The banging and ringing stopped. A man's voice said "Brszfrsk." I said, "Who is it?" again. The voice said, "Mfmdnsk!" "I can't hear you!" I called.

My mother appeared in her robe, which she'd buttoned wrong, her face looking like she wasn't really awake. "What's going on, Neil?" she said in this voice that sounded like it was coming from down in a well. "What's happening?"

"Someone's out there—" I pointed at the door.

"At this hour?" My mother started waking up. She went to the door. "Who is it?" she said.

"Frtrskd!" said the voice.

"What do you want?" said my mother.

"FRTRSKD!"

My mother opened the door a crack, just the length of the chain, and we both peeked out.

Mr. Rasmussen! He was standing there in a blue-and-white striped bathrobe and a pair of slippers. His Scottie dog was not with him.

"You took the telephone off the hook!" he said. He was red in the face.

"I'm sorry—" my mother started to say. "I took a sleeping pill—"

"I'm up half the night listening to the drumming on the walls, the pounding, the crashing, and now—" his face got even redder, sort of like instant sunburn—"you expect me to put up with the piano at five in the morning?"

"What happened was—" I started to say, but he cut me right off.

"I hardly slept twenty minutes since eleven o'clock last night!"

My mother tried to tell him again that she was sorry, but he wouldn't let her finish a sentence.

"I've had it up to here!" he said. He made a sign with his hands like he was going to cut his head off at the neck. "Up to here!" he said, and without another word, he turned on his heel and marched off, his slippers slapping against the corridor floor.

My father had come into the living room, had heard the last few of Mr. Rasmussen's remarks, and now flopped himself into a chair and stared at the floor.

My mother closed the door and turned to look at him. "Poor man, I can hardly blame him," she said.

"He's going to make trouble for us, Margery," my father said.

"What can he do?" I asked.

"I don't know," my mother said.

"Plenty," my father said.

When I got to school I got the shock of my life. The minute I walked into home room, the teacher called me right to his desk. "Don't go to your first-period class. You're to go directly to Mr. Guttag's office. He's waiting for you."

Waiting for me? Good, grey grief! Hadn't Beef fixed that cut slip? Waiting for me! Those words had an end-of-the-world ring that took the wind right out of me. The principal of the school, stopping everything to wait for *me!*

I made my way down to his office, but I practically had to hold on to the walls. My legs felt so weak, it was like I'd been sick with the flu for a week and was now allowed out of bed for the first time. I held on to the bannisters going downstairs and tried to take deep breaths for courage. I found out that taking deep breaths for courage doesn't work.

Mr. Guttag's secretary hardly looked up from her typewriter when I came in. "Sit down and Mr. Guttag will be with you in a minute," she said.

I sat and imagined what was in store for me, a

second offender. I imagined the screams that would come out of Mr. Guttag's throat, the punishments he would invent for me. "Go in now," the secretary said, too soon. My stomach jumped right up into my throat. Another kid had just left Guttag's office and I wondered about him. He didn't look as if anything too awful had happened. On the other hand, he wasn't smiling either.

I went straight into the office and stood in front of Mr. Guttag's desk. He put down the cut slip he'd been reading like it was his favorite book and stared at me for what seemed like ten years. "Okay, Oxley, what's the matter?"

I didn't know what to answer, so I didn't answer.

"Did you hear me? What's wrong?"

"Nothing, Mr. Guttag."

"You were in here a couple of days ago for causing a disturbance in Mrs. Bowring's class. *What is the matter with you, boy?* Is something wrong at home?"

How was I going to answer that one? I didn't answer. I looked at the little golf club paperweight holding down the papers on his desk and I swallowed a couple of times. I kept thinking how Beef had taken my dollar and flim-flammed me but good.

"This school has a strict cutting policy. Are you aware of it, Oxley?"

I said I was aware of it.

"Then why did you cut English class?"

"I didn't have my report."

"*And why didn't you have your report, may I ask?*"

"It got messed up."

"Messed up?"

I shut right up, I don't know why. It would have been impossible to tell him about Gerri. If I told him about Gerri, he'd call my mother and father and make a big thing. Then for all I know they'd send Gerri back to the Training Center. Did I want that on my conscience?

"I'm not going to waste any more time. I'm going to suspend you from classes today. You'll sit right in that chair in the outer office until it's time to go home at three o'clock. You may leave only to go to the cafeteria during fifth period for half an hour, to eat your lunch."

I got up and moved to the outer office thinking that there was absolutely no reason for me to go to the cafeteria for lunch since it was almost a sure thing I'd never be able to eat even one bite.

But I did go to the cafeteria during fifth period and it was one of the biggest mistakes I'd ever made in my life. It got me into even worse trouble than I was in already—and if Mr. Guttag was tough with second offenders, he was practically frothing at the mouth the third time around!

fourteen

I ADMIT THAT BY THE TIME LUNCH PERIOD CAME around, I did want to eat, although I didn't do much in Mr. Guttag's office to build up an appetite. Mostly I just watched Mr. Guttag's secretary type and answer the telephone and saw who went into Mr. Guttag's office, and what they looked like when he let them out. (Pale, mostly.)

About eleven o'clock another kid got suspended for calling his math teacher a weirdo, and he and I played Tic-Tac-Toe for a while and it wasn't that bad. In fact, the kid said tomorrow he was going to call his home-room teacher a weirdo to make sure he'd get another day off. I told him I might cut again so we could continue our game, but I really didn't mean it. No kidding, I never wanted to be suspended again.

We were sent out to lunch at about twelve o'clock, and by that time my mouth was watering for the Friday special, cheese pizza. I got on the cafeteria line and was waiting my turn when I spotted Beef Adams having lunch at a table with a bunch of his East End buddies.

It was like somebody stuck an ice cube down the back of my T-shirt. Just seeing him sitting there laughing with his friends, probably telling them what a fast one he'd pulled on the big chumpo in his English class, gave me a chill. Seeing him eating his pizzas (no kidding, he had one in front of him on a plate and one in his hand) was ruining my appetite, especially when I figured I'd paid for one of them. I left the line and made a beeline over to his table.

"Okay, Beef," I said, trying to sound like I was tougher and meaner than Mr. Guttag and might even be carrying a knife or a hand grenade in my pocket. "Give me back my dollar."

Beef looked around at his friends and winked at one of them before he answered me. That made me even madder. "What dollar?" said Beef. One of his finks laughed.

"The dollar I gave you yesterday, for fixing the cut slip you didn't fix, Adams."

"I spent it. I bet it on the Yankees. Sorry, they lost." All his friends went *ha ha ha* like they never heard anything so funny.

"Give me back the dollar, Adams."

"I told you, the Yankees lost. Bug off if you don't want to be a loser too." *Ha ha ha.*

"I want my dollar and I want it now."

"Hey, didn't you hear me?" Beef said. "Didn't you understand what I told you?" he said, and then he said something that made the red flag go up. "What are you, retarded or something? Does it run in your family?"

It was like he stuck my finger into an electric wall socket. I went berserk. I picked the extra pizza off his plate, lifted it into the air, and mashed it right into his face. It caught the right side of his head, and no kidding, it actually made me feel good to see the tomato sauce and cheese running out of his ear.

Of course, he went wild. He threw the other pizza right back at me and caught my left shoulder and neck. Then he picked up his milk container and hurled it too, but I ducked and it hit a pole and sprayed a girl wearing glasses who was sitting next to it. She just sat there with milk covering both lenses and running down her nose, looking ghostly and not knowing what hit her.

The entire cafeteria went wild.

The screaming was like in a football stadium. Beef's friends were pounding the table yelling "GO! GO! GO!" like he was going to make a touchdown. Other kids were stomping their feet and leaping on the tables; an applauding, whistling crowd was gathering.

It didn't last long. Within a minute, I saw Mr. Peck, the assistant principal, zigzagging toward us, his face looking like a death mask in the art museum. It was all over before you could say Reform School. "Let's go, fellas, the party's over," he said, and I didn't have to ask where we were going. I just wished that a hand would reach down from the sky—maybe Grandpa's, but I didn't really care whose—and grab me up out of the cafeteria, out of this school, and dump me somewhere else, preferably as far away from Mr. Guttag as possible, like Venus or Saturn.

None of that happened. Mr. Peck knew the way to Mr. Guttag's office so well that we arrived there before I could finish even half of the Lord's Prayer. I was at "give us this day our daily bread" when Mr. Peck pushed us in our same old seats and told us not to move an inch. The secretary stopped typing and looked up over her glasses at us.

Before I could even get to "those who trespass against us," Mr. Guttag's face, carried on his familiar body, made its way right toward us. I actually wished Gerri were here right now, to go over and throw her arms around him, change his expression from murderous to at least not-so-murderous, maybe soften his eyes from tombstone grey to just plain grey.

No luck. We were led to his office one by one, Beef first, then me, and I think stake-burning would have been easier. The inquisition lasted forever. What was wrong with me, he wanted to know. Did I realize that I was in danger of being expelled? "Expelled" was a word I put in the same category as "electric chair." Things like that didn't happen to people in my family, or hadn't, until now.

At the very minute that thought fluttered through my head like a dark and terrible bat, Mr. Guttag leaned back in his chair, stretched his lips above his teeth to make sure I could see he had none missing, and asked me what I thought my parents would say when they found out that I had caused a near-riot in the cafeteria. Would they be proud of a son who had assaulted another boy with a pizza without any provocation?

Since I didn't want to tell him about the provocation, I couldn't think of an answer for that question. What was more, I knew if I'd had another pizza and some more time, I'd have thrown one at Joe/Jason too, for blabbing it all over school about Gerri. At the same time, I didn't even want to think about what would happen when my mother and father found out. I even—believe it or not—thought it might be a relief to find a wall to bang my own head against to get some of the terrible it's-going-to-burst feeling out of it.

"What will they say when I tell them you've been sent to my office three times in the last three days? That you behaved in a violent and dangerous way?"

"I don't think they'll like it." Here was the understatement of all understatements. I managed to say it, but not very loud.

"Well, let's find out," said Mr. Guttag.

To my absolute horror, it turned out that Mr. Guttag was going to call my mother this very minute, while I was still sitting here, waiting for the hand from the sky to rescue me, and dying of fright a mile a minute.

Instead of a hand from the sky, Mr. Guttag's secretary appeared with a card with who-knows-what written on it. Mr. Guttag studied the card a few seconds and then he looked up at me. "Your father's name is Theodore?"

"Yes," I said. Nobody ever calls my father anything but Ted, although his mail is addressed to Theodore. Maybe Mr. Guttag just intended to send a letter to my father instead of calling?

No. His hand was reaching for the telephone; I guess our telephone number was written on the card too.

Had they called Beef's house too? Beef had left Mr. Guttag's office looking smug, giving me a big wink on his way past my chair as if he'd just gotten away with everything, had pinned it all on me, and was now getting the afternoon off to celebrate.

While Mr. Guttag waited for my mother to answer the telephone, he looked at me with his I'll-get-you eyes and drummed on his desk blotter with his fingers.

"Hello," he finally said, and my stomach did a complete somersault—I moved to the edge of the chair in case I had to run out of his office to the boys' room to throw up.

"Mrs. Oxley?" he said, and there was a pause. "I see. When will she be in?"

He'd gotten Mrs. Shrub! I'd forgotten that Mrs. Shrub had promised to stay with Gerri so my mother could go to the beauty parlor to have her hair cut, although today, Friday, was not Mrs. Shrub's regular day.

"Will you have her call Mr. Guttag at Franklin Pierce Junior High School the minute she comes in, please? And please tell her I'm delaying Neil at school until I hear from her."

"Delaying Neil" meant I was a prisoner in this office, until who knows when my mother would get home.

"I hope your mother calls early. I have an appointment in the city and have to leave school at five," Mr. Guttag said, looking at his watch.

Five! The tryouts were at three! I moved back in my chair, looked up at the clock over Mr. Guttag's office door, and began to wait. It was 2:05. I crossed my fingers; how long could a haircut take?

What I never expected and what really surprised me was that my mother never called at all and that I not only lost my chance to try out for the Follies, but I lost something much more important as well.

fifteen

It was my father who got the message from Mrs. Shrub, and he didn't bother calling the school, he just came right over. It was almost five o'clock and I'd long since missed the tryouts and was sitting in Mr. Guttag's office watching his secretary cover her typewriter when my father came in. He saw the tomato sauce from the pizza on my shirt first and must have thought it was blood; he looked really scared for a minute. "What's happened to you, Neil?" he asked. "Who did that to you?"

"Mr. Oxley?" Mr. Guttag came out of his office and he looked altogether different when he was talking to my father. He didn't look like he was going to throw punches or beat someone up with leather straps. He looked like somebody who might work at a bank or some other place ordinary people work who don't have to push kids around to make a living.

He almost looked as if he were going to smile, but instead he simply asked us both to come into his office and put us each in a chair, only this time it was more like we were going to have a tea party instead of a neck-wringing.

Even so, my father looked very uncomfortable, pulling at his shirt, his tie, and his belt, as if everything he had on was too tight. "Is this very serious?" he asked Mr. Guttag.

"I wouldn't have called your home if it weren't serious, Mr. Oxley," Mr. Guttag said. He leaned back in his chair so far I was afraid he was going to tip over and bang his head on the plant on the window sill behind him. "Mr. Oxley, your son assaulted another boy today," Mr. Guttag said. I know it's nothing to be proud of, but he made it sound like a hatchet murder.

My father's eyebrows went up. "It doesn't sound like Neil," he said.

Mr. Guttag looked at me. "He caused a terrible commotion in the cafeteria. My assistant principal, Mr. Peck, had a most difficult time restoring peace. Furthermore, this is the third time this week Neil has been sent to my office."

Now my father's eyebrows really went up. "I'm surprised," he said. "Really surprised. You never told us, Neil," he said, turning to me.

I looked at the floor, then I looked at the little golf club on Mr. Guttag's desk. Mr. Guttag picked up the card that had my telephone number and, as it turned out, all my sins listed on it, and he began reading. "He had a scuffle in Mrs. Bowring's English class Wednesday. He cut that same class yesterday, and today, even though he was suspended, and apparently with very little provocation, he attacked another boy with a pizza."

"Mr. Guttag, I assure you, I couldn't be more surprised," my father said. "Neil has never been a problem in school or at home. If you check with his last school, you'll be convinced that he has a spotless record, without any discipline reports."

Mr. Guttag listened to my father sticking up for me, and he looked very thoughtful. A couple of times he nodded and glanced in my direction. Then he picked up his little golf club to fiddle with, and cleared his throat.

"Is there a special problem here at school, Neil? Is something bothering you?" He had taken the spikes out of his voice and sounded . . . well, almost friendly.

I said nothing was bothering me.

Then Mr. Guttag turned to my father. "Could there be a problem at home?" he said.

My father cleared his throat and he lifted his hand to his moustache and he rubbed his fingers back and forth across it a couple of times. A big silence fell into the office like rain.

"There is a problem," my father finally said, kind of slowly. "With Neil's sister." His voice was funny, like it was going over bumps.

Mr. Guttag seemed very alert now. He squinted down at the card with my telephone number on it, as if he were going to find a sister listed in with the sins, and then he turned back to my father. He said, "We don't seem to have her listed here." He picked up a ball-point pen and aimed it at the card. "Older sister or younger sister?" he said.

"That's the problem," my father said, and then he said it again. "That's the problem."

Mr. Guttag looked at me, and he looked at my father, who wasn't saying much of anything else. "Is it something we can discuss?" he finally asked.

My father said, "I'd like to discuss it, yes. Neil, would you step out of the office for a minute, please?"

Why my father wanted to make a world-war spy secret out of Geraldine, I don't know. If everybody else would just keep cool and give her a chance to fit into the world better, she'd be fine. If she didn't think people were waiting to jump all over her for making mistakes, and would maybe try harder to listen to her reindeer talk and wouldn't point at her in the street and run away from her in the park, she'd stop crashing her head into walls and pulling curtains off windows.

I couldn't hear what my father was saying through the closed door, but I did hear his voice and Mr. Guttag's voice, and here and there, I understood a word or a sentence. One part of a sentence I heard got my ears up. It was louder than the rest of the conversation and it came from my father. "My wife refuses—" I heard him say, and I tried to figure out for myself what came next. "Refuses to send her back to the school"? or maybe, "Refuses to give her up"?

I guess I was glad I wasn't in there listening; I didn't want to hear any of it. I just sat there in my chair drawing flags of the world on my notebook, waiting for my father to come out and take me home. Maybe I'd ask him to take us out to Lake Alfred for the weekend—I could show Gerri how to fish if we could get an extra pole; she might like that. But just as I had the thought, the office door opened, my father stepped out, and I could tell in a second by his face that he was in no mood for fishing.

He shook hands with Mr. Guttag, and Mr. Guttag came over to me and, no kidding, put his arm around my shoulder! I was nearly knocked over by surprise. He said he knew I'd be making no more trouble at Franklin Pierce Junior High and could see I was under what he called "stress" at home and said he understood perfectly. It all translated into his feeling sorry for me to have Gerri for a sister, but there was no setting him straight. He'd probably never even met anyone like her, so I don't think he could understand perfectly. I don't think he could really understand at all.

On the way home my father and I had a serious talk. Actually, it was my father who talked. I listened. He told me that he understood how my sister was disrupting my life, because she was disrupting his life, too. He said he himself was very, very upset and didn't know what exactly could be done. He said that we were not going to continue living this way, that was for sure. I asked him what he meant and he didn't answer.

Suddenly, he remembered the tryouts. "Did you play well? Did you make mistakes? How did you do?" he asked.

Of course, I had to tell him I'd been sitting in Mr. Guttag's office the whole afternoon and had missed them.

"Well, they'll certainly let you try out Monday if you explain the circumstances, won't they?" my father wanted to know. I think he was more upset about my missing the chance to play in the Follies than he was about my throwing the pizza at Beef.

I said no, they were choosing the piano player today. In my heart I guess I knew I didn't have a chance against Wendy Wellington anyway.

Maybe I shouldn't have told him the bad news right then. I think it was too much for my father. A couple of weeks later, he moved out.

sixteen

WHAT HAPPENED WAS THAT FOR A LONG TIME MY FA-
ther couldn't get "Firecracker in My Heart" written
the way he wanted it. The refrain was great but the
release never sounded right, and he said he could
never concentrate enough to get good lyrics for the
last eight bars with Gerri around. This time he
wanted to make sure the song was recorded and
the deal did not fall through, so very often after
dinner he'd have to leave the apartment to go to
his friend's house, where there was peace and
quiet and no Geraldine.

One afternoon, when my mother was out and I
was in my room, my father came home early.
"Anybody home?" he called the minute he opened
the front door, and right away I could tell he was
in a holiday mood. Gerri and I both came running
immediately; that Fourth of July sound in his voice
meant something good was up.

"Hiya, Neil! Hiya, Gerri!" he said, and he practically zipped across the living room to the piano, pulled his "Firecracker" music out of the bench and set it on the music stand, then plopped himself on the bench and loosened his tie. "I think I really have it, Neil!" he said. "Right in the middle of a phone call from Cincinnati when I was quoting the market price for IBM, it just flew into my head from nowhere. I better put it down quick before it gets away!"

My father doesn't get excited often, but he was really excited now. He opened the piano, tilted his head, and began to play. He played about three chords, then he stopped. He looked down at the keys, touched a couple of them and tried another chord, "What the devil is all over these keys?" he asked.

I went over and looked at the keys. I touched a couple of them. "They're sticky," I said.

"What from? What are they sticky from?" my father said. The Fourth of July went right out of his voice and the holiday expression disappeared from his face.

I figured applesauce, but it didn't matter; we both knew they were sticky from Gerri, that it was Gerri who had messed up the piano, that it was Gerri, again and again, who was fouling things up, snafuing everything.

My father got up from the bench and stalked into the kitchen. I followed him; I guess I wanted to help clean up the keys so he could hurry and get started before he lost all the stuff that had come into his head during his phone call from Cincinnati. I rushed around and found a sponge, and he held it under the warm-water tap until it was soft enough to use, and I found the Ivory soap he told me to look for and then followed him back into the living room, and oh, good, grey grief, Gerri was sitting on the piano bench and just lifting a crayon to the firecracker music, pretending to write notes all over it like my father does.

My father flew to the piano and got there just in time to grab the crayon out of Gerri's hand, before she'd messed up the whole page. Then he threw the sponge on the floor and he yelled at her.

Gerri started to scream and my father just stood there with his face turning redder and redder, holding on to the sheet music like it was a breathing baby and no kidding, his hand was shaking like there were no muscles or bones in it.

Finally, he pulled his eyebrows toward each other as if there was a stripe of horrible pain right behind them and he shook his head. "I've lost it, Neil," he said to me, and he made a fist with his hand and held it up to his mouth the way people do when they are trying to keep their hands warm. Then he slumped onto the piano bench and shook his head. "It's gone," he whispered.

Ten minutes later he was in the bedroom packing the suitcase he'd brought out of the storage room; it was the same suitcase we'd used to bring Gerri's stuff home from the training school.

Gerri was standing in the door of the bedroom, holding Woodie and watching. My father was opening drawers, pulling out socks and underwear and shirts, and stuffing them into the suitcase. His face was still red and his hands were still shaking.

"I've thought about this a long time, Neil," he was saying. "A long time. It's nothing sudden. The situation here—it's not good," he said. I could see he was perspiring. His forehead was wet and a drop of wetness was moving down the side of his head in a straight line to his chin. "As soon as I get another apartment set up, I want you to think about coming to live with me. I think it's important for a boy of your age to have a peaceful home life without the sort of . . . pressures we're living under here."

"Dad, I don't mind," I started to say, but even as I was saying it, Gerri had shuffled into the bedroom and begun opening dresser drawers and pulling out clothes and trying to stuff them into the open suitcase. I suppose I would have thought it was funny to see her pulling my mother's bras and pantyhose out of the drawers and think she was helping, but my father didn't think it was funny at all. I think he'd had enough. He just threw a ball of socks on the bed like he hoped the socks would put a hole right through the mattress and he yelled, "GERALDINE, STOP IT!" in a dragon voice that could shatter eardrums and must have traveled through three floors.

Geraldine's eyes opened wide and her mouth opened wider. She looked as if she'd peeked into a jack-in-the-box and a fiend had jumped out. Then, oh, good, grey grief, she wet her pants. I looked down at the rug where she was standing and saw this awful dark spot that was getting bigger and darker and right away I could see that my father hadn't missed it either.

He just walked out of the room and I heard him open the piano bench and clean out the music. He came back to stuff it all into his suitcase. Then he snapped the case shut and picked it up.

"I'm going to leave it up to you, Neil, I know you'll make a wise decision," he said, and he went into the living room, wrote a short note to my mother, pushed it into an envelope, pasted it shut, and gave it to me to give to her. "I'll call you soon," he said and he set down the suitcase and put both his arms around me. Then he just held me and held me and I thought maybe he was thinking it over and changing his mind and would go right back in the bedroom and unpack and just stay here with us like always. Instead, he just gave me one more squeeze and ran his hand over his eyes, and then he picked up his suitcase and walked out of the apartment for good.

Without my saying a word, my mother could see something was wrong the minute she came home. She put down her packages so she could read the note my father had given me to give her, and she went over to the kitchen doorway and leaned against it when she opened the envelope.

Gerri had learned a new word, something that sounded like "Womba," which turned out to mean Mama. As soon as she saw Mom come in, she started saying, "Womba, Womba," because she was not only thrilled to see her mother come home but also seemed pleased with herself for improving her vocabulary. So while Mom read the note, Gerri kept yelling "Womba, Womba, Womba" at the top of her lungs.

I said, "Ssshh, Gerri, shh," really wishing I could stuff a couple of handkerchiefs in her mouth the way the crooks do on TV when they really want to shut somebody up, but I didn't want to upset my mother any more than she was already upset. So Gerri kept it up—*Womba, Womba*—sounding like a caveman about to throw a spear. I was watching my mother; her nose was getting red and she was pressing her lips together very tight. All of a sudden, she ran into the bathroom and shut the door; a minute later I heard water running. My heart felt like it was going *womba womba* too.

But she came out almost right away looking okay. She told me she wasn't really surprised that Dad had left. I told her exactly what had happened and she said she didn't blame my father, not one bit. Then she took Geraldine into the bathroom to clean her up and said that life was just going to have to go on and that we'd better start thinking about preparing dinner. She asked me to wash four baking potatoes and stick them in the oven. Then she quickly said, "Not four baking potatoes, I mean *three* baking potatoes," and she started to cry, and no kidding, it was awful.

I felt like running out of the apartment and going somewhere else like the laundry room or the garage or out on the street, maybe trying to find my father and make him come back, asking him to think it over, *please*. But instead I just went into the living room.

Almost immediately I could tell something was different. The piano bench was open and empty, except for a few of my Chopin exercise books and a few old songbooks, but there was something else missing.

Then I realized what it was. My father had taken the big photograph of Grandpa with him, and mine was gone too. The only picture left on top of the piano now was Gerri's, the one my mother had taken with the Polaroid and put in the white leather frame. It was standing on the piano all by itself. My father had left that one behind.

seventeen

AFTER MY FATHER LEFT, EVERYTHING WENT SORT OF dim. My mother spent a lot of time in her bedroom with the door closed and little things began to bother her that had never bothered her before. If one of us spilled anything, she'd lose her temper and let us have it. Then she'd feel awful and spend half an hour apologizing to me or to Gerri. We couldn't afford Mrs. Shrub any more, so my mother and I took turns vacuuming and I helped her change the bedsheets and lug stuff to the basement laundry room. If I took Gerri down with me I'd have to watch her every minute or she'd pour a half a box of soap in someone else's machine or go up to anyone and give him one of her out-of-the-blue-sky hugs. Gerri was finally getting used to the elevator, but if it lurched, or too many people got on, she'd want to get out right away; she once scared the daylights out of a couple who were visiting someone on the fifth floor by letting out a shriek when they tried to roll a baby carriage in.

Her head-banging got worse after my father left, and pretty often my mother would fall asleep in Gerri's room with Gerri on her lap and I'd find her sitting there asleep in the morning. Now, aside from the telephone calls neighbors made to complain, and their pounding on the walls, we'd get notes slipped in our mailbox or under the door. The notes were full of awful words.

Finally, one afternoon, Mr. Parrish called. My mother was out shopping with Gerri because Gerri needed sneakers; my mother had promised to buy her any pair she picked as a reward for learning how to tie her own shoelaces.

Just hearing Mr. Parrish's voice on the telephone again was enough to give me the glacier chills. If he wanted to talk to my mother this time, I knew it had to be about us leaving the apartment. If he was calling to tell us to pack up and get out, where would we live?

I supposed I could go live with my father, but where would my mother and Gerri go? My father called pretty often and he always wanted to know if I was playing the piano and was I practicing enough? I didn't even tell him I'd stopped taking lessons; I just told him the good news, which was that I was playing more than ever. It was the truth; I did like fiddling around at the piano if I didn't have to do scales and all the boring études. After I'd gotten "You Have a Lovely Baby Boy" down pat, I taught myself to play the Battle Hymn of the Republic—which was the best of the numbers Wendy Wellington was going to be playing in the Follies—and when Gerri climbed up on the piano, to tell the truth, as long as she took off her shoes, I just let her. She'd sit up there not bothering anybody, just to listen, and she seemed to like my playing a lot. It was the one time you could bet your life she'd be quiet and not get in anybody's way.

On the day Mr. Parrish called, in she came, wearing her new sneakers, which were really cool, and looked a lot like a couple of the flags of the world I have all over my notebook (Italy and Great Britain), only better. My mother looked pooped but she was smiling: Gerri had learned two new words—*shoe* and *sock*—and had practiced saying them all the way home. Gerri sat on the couch next to my mother and looked really pleased with herself. She smiled down at her sneakers and said, "Shew, sock, sock, shew. Sock sock shew shew."

She looked much better these days because my mother made her sleep with two wool scarfs tied around her head so the bumps would stop bumping out no matter how hard she banged. She was almost all healed up and her hair was growing in, and when it was all combed down flat and her face was clean, she looked something like Jane Reilly, who is playing Betsy Ross in the Follies and got the part because she is so pretty.

I wanted to put off telling my mother about Mr.

Parrish, but I couldn't. I knew she'd boggle like I did just hearing he wanted to come up to talk to her, and sure enough, she got up from the couch and began walking around the room, not really looking at anything, just rubbing her elbows as if she were putting cream on them, and pacing from the windows to the door, and back to the windows again.

I wanted her to tell me it would be all right, that if Mr. Parrish didn't want us living in his building we'd find another place just as good, but she had a look on her face that said I-don't-want-to-talk-about-it. I guess she was thinking what I was thinking. If a good guy like Mr. Parrish didn't want Gerri in his building, who would?

When he came up to the apartment this time, it was after dinner and we were watching television in my mother's room, so it was no problem keeping Gerri out of the living room. She had her eyes glued to the TV because she loves to watch people dance and sing, and luck was with me; channel four had a great musical review rerun and she wasn't taking her eyes off it.

I left her in there and stood in the hall near the door to the living room where I could hear what was going on. Then right away I was sorry I was listening because I didn't like any of what I was hearing.

"You know I'm sorry, Mrs. Oxley," Mr. Parrish was saying. I heard the rustle of paper. Was it the lease? Was he going to tear it up into little pieces and throw it out the window like confetti or do some other marble-hearted thing?

It wasn't the lease, though. It was a petition. I heard him tell my mother, "Eight tenants have signed this petition, Mrs. Oxley," and I heard my mother cry out like she was having a bad middle-of-the-night dream, "I can't send her back! I just can't!"

To which Mr. Parrish said, "There isn't much I can do."

I couldn't see my mother and I couldn't hear her very well either. She did say something else, but I don't know what it was. As for me, I felt like a wrecking ball was swinging at my life.

Eight people in the building had passed around a paper asking Mr. Parrish to get us out, not let us live in our own apartment any more, *get rid of us.* I imagined them passing the petition from door to door, getting everybody to run around looking for a ball-point pen to sign it with, happy to be doing something that would help rid the building of a pest like Gerri, like she was a termite chewing up the foundation.

I stood there in the dark hall and no kidding, I felt that hitting the wall with my head wouldn't be enough; I wanted to kick everything in sight, write rotten words on the walls, break windows like some of the East End kids did every day of the week. I wanted to grab Gerri by the hand and drag her around through the building and show every-body that she was no termite and was learning new stuff every day—like not getting the tooth-paste all over the sink and always remembering to flush the toilet and eating cheeseburgers without waiting for applesauce.

If I couldn't take her around from door to door, at least I thought I could show her to Mr. Parrish, ask her to say "shew" and "sock," and make sure he saw that she wasn't pulling down the curtains and the curtain rods or screeching in the elevator any more.

When I heard Mr. Parrish telling my mother that he was going to ask us to be out by the first of next month, I figured I had to drag Gerri out there to show how far she'd come, what a good citizen she was turning into, and how if people would only give her a chance, they'd see she was a person like everybody else even if she was a bit of a variation.

I ran into the bedroom and grabbed her hand. "Come on, Gerri," I said, "I want you to go in there and say 'shew' and 'sock' to Mr. Parrish."

Would you believe she wouldn't budge? A bunch of ladies with colored umbrellas were doing Japanese dances on channel four and Gerri wasn't going to move away from the set and miss a bit of it. She was sitting there with Woodie on her lap, her eyes glommed on the screen like she'd never seen anything in her life this interesting. I just stood there thinking how I'd like to give her a nice punch, or one killer-karate chop—*whap*. That would get her really moving fast. Or I could zap her with one of her own sneakers. Mom would never have to know.

Hey, sneakers. I eyed Gerri's new ones, which she'd slipped off her feet when she sat on the bed to watch the show. I scooped them up and ran out of the room with them, intending to show Mr. Parrish how my mother had worked and worked to get her to make a knot and tie a bow and finally gotten her to be pretty good at it. I arrived in the living room just as Mr. Parrish was leaving. My mother was slumped into a chair staring at the floor, and he was about to go to the front door when I flew in with the sneakers.

"Look, Mr. Parrish," I said, and I held them practically up to his nose in the foyer so he could see how well Gerri had tied the knots and how even she'd managed to get the laces. "My mother taught my sister to tie her own shoelaces," I said. I was out of breath from the dash I'd made and at first I thought Mr. Parrish hadn't understood what I'd said. His face stayed sort of blank as if he were watching a movie with the sound turned off and wasn't getting it, so I told him again. "My sister learned how to tie these all by herself," I said.

He had heard and he had understood. The bad news was that he didn't really care that Gerri had learned to tie her own shoelaces. He didn't get it, how Gerri was on her way up.

He had that petition in his hand and I guess his mind was set, fixed, and frozen against us. He said, "That's very nice, Neil," in an I'll-be-polite voice, and then he turned away from me, leaving me standing there with the sneakers hanging in my hand like a couple of too-small fish I had to throw back in the river.

"Shews, shews," We both spun around. I guessed the Japanese ladies had stopped dancing, because Gerri was shuffling towards us, smiling from ear to ear, heading right for Mr. Parrish and saying "Shews, shews." Then, just as she was practically on top of us, she did the most incredible thing!

She walked right up to Mr. Parrish and held out her hand, waiting to shake!

No kidding, shake hands instead of hug!

When had my mother finally gotten it through Gerri's head that she wasn't to throw her arms around and squeeze everybody she ran into? When had she taught her that shaking hands was polite and grown-up and civilized and didn't scare people out of their wits?

I guess that really surprised Mr. Parrish. He just held out his right hand and Gerri took it and they shook and it was very serious and solemn, like they weren't just shaking hands, but making a big-time deal.

All of a sudden, his whole face changed; he looked like someone on the highest diving board who suddenly gets too scared to make the dive. Then he said something about losing his job but having to live with his own conscience, and—would you believe it—he took the petition in his two hands and tore it straight across once and then twice, and he handed the pieces to Gerri, and he patted her hair where it had grown back in, and without another word to me or my mother, he turned and walked out of the apartment.

My mother and I were so relieved that Gerri had saved our apartment again, we just took one look at each other and burst out laughing, especially my mother, who needed three tissues to wipe her eyes and blow her nose.

I went over and shook Gerri's hand all over again and promised to teach her to say thank you and how to play a C scale, but as it turned out, "thank you" was too hard for Gerri to say, and teaching her to play a C scale was impossible because when I got home from school a couple of days later, the piano was gone.

eighteen

DAD HAD THE PIANO REMOVED WHEN MY MOTHER LET it slip I'd stopped taking lessons. She said it took a whole morning and part of the afternoon for the men to take it apart and lift it out of the windows. In a way I'm glad it happened when I was at school.

I admit it, I missed the piano. School had turned worse than ever because now I wouldn't even speak to Joe/Jason. I figured that any kid who had blabbed to Beef about Geraldine was not my friend, even though he tried to tell me about a zillion times that it had accidentally just slipped out of him to two East-Enders in science class, when the teacher was talking about extra chromosomes. I thought I might forgive him in five or ten years, but I wasn't ready to forgive him now; I just wandered around school alone most of the time, feeling like a flea without a dog.

Until one day when I wandered into the auditorium right after school. It was empty, there was a gorgeous concert grand piano just standing there waiting for someone to play it, and I was in no hurry to get home to look at the big empty space in the living room where our own Bechstein had been.

I sat down and did a few scales just to get my fingers limber, and then I slid into a few chords, an arpeggio, and on into the Battle Hymn of the Republic, and I guess I was halfway through when I realized I had an audience.

A whole bunch of kids from the music/drama group had come into the auditorium, probably to rehearse for the Follies, and had been standing there listening to me play without my even realizing it. Of course, I stopped cold and just sat there feeling like I was winning a blushing contest, not knowing what to do and not knowing what to say.

"Hey, don't stop now!" somebody called to me from the back, and no kidding, I'm not sure what came over me, but not knowing exactly what else to do, I just started again where I'd left off and went through the whole piece better than I'd ever played it, with only one baby mistake that no one but Wendy Wellington could have picked up.

She was there too, of course; I saw her watching me from the stage exit and when I finished, she started the applause. By this time I felt like my face had gone to the color of tomato soup, so I jumped up from the bench and said, "I gotta go now," and

I ran out of there past all those kids like I had to rush off to be on time for an appointment with the President of the United States. As I ran out of the auditorium, I heard Joe/Jason's voice call after me, "Neil, hey, Neil! Come back here, willya?" but I kept running and running until I was out on the street and by myself, where I guess I felt I belonged.

That night, Dad picked me up in the ord and drove me out to Lake Alfred for the weekend. We had a great time fishing Saturday and I caught one small and one pretty good-size rainbow trout and a sunfish we had to throw back. On Sunday it rained most of the morning, so Dad and I sat in the cabin after breakfast looking at the rain run down the windows, and I guess it made us both sad, because Dad got into one of his silent moods and I didn't feel much like talking either.

When it let up after lunch, I said I was going for a little hike around the lake to look for early raspberries. I was hoping Dad would come with me, but he was sitting in the living room rocker with yesterday's newspaper in his lap and said to go right ahead, he'd see me when I got back; he'd just stay here and take it easy. I set off with an empty tin can and didn't give it another thought, because I never expected the surprise that was waiting for me when I got back.

The whole hike was pretty much of a disaster, not only because it turned out to be much too early for raspberries, but also because when I'd gotten halfway around the lake it started to rain again. It rained hard enough to get me soaked through to the skin and kept me busy trying to avoid stepping into mud puddles that looked bigger than moon craters, and the whole hike took about three times longer than I'd expected it to.

Dad wasn't in the living room when I got back, and he wasn't on the porch either. I went into the bathroom to dry off and I found an open razor lying on the sink. I was really puzzled because Dad doesn't use anything but an electric shaver. It scared me a little too. I guess I've seen a thousand horror movies that use razors for bloody murder and suicide weapons and it got me jittery and wondering—where was Dad, anyway?

"You back, Neil?" His voice came from the kitchen, sounding safe and unmurdered. A minute later his face appeared in the doorway. "Did you get caught in that downpour?" he said.

I nearly jumped a foot. Good, grey grief, Dad had shaved off his moustache! No kidding, I was speechless. It was gone. His face was back, and it was the last thing I expected. Dad had really loved his moustache. I'd seen him at the mirror a hundred times trimming it and brushing it, smoothing it down and even shampooing it. It had taken him so long to get it full and thick, the way he wanted it.

"Why'd you shave it off, Dad?" I asked. "How come?"

Dad sort of shrugged the way he does when some little thing goes wrong, like a fuse blowing or the fishing line getting tangled around the rod, and he said, "It was uncomfortable, Neil, darned uncomfortable. It was getting on my nerves so I thought, why not get rid of it? and I found this old razor up in the medicine chest and—*fffft*—no more moustache, see?"

It took a while getting used to a moustacheless Dad, but by the time he got me home I decided that although I liked his face better with a moustache, it wasn't bad plain either. He stopped in front of our building, and now that he was double-parked, he got talkative. He said he was sorry about taking the piano but he really needed it. He said he'd finished "Firecracker" and wanted me to come to his new apartment to hear him play it. Then he got very serious and said he wanted me to think over moving in with him as soon as possible. All the while he was talking I kept thinking that now that his face was so different maybe he'd come home again to live. I guess all along I'd thought that his moving out wasn't going to be forever and that one day when I woke up in the morning, he'd be in the living room sitting on the piano bench like always.

"I wouldn't really want to leave Mom and Gerri," I said, and my father turned away from me and looked through the windshield, although there was nothing out there to see.

I thought that maybe I should tell him how my

mother sometimes does the same thing, stands looking out of the window for an hour at a time at nothing at all, and how she burst into tears for no reason day before yesterday when she dropped a bottle of shampoo in the bathroom and it broke.

Instead I said, "Gerri is learning to talk. She can say 'shoe' and 'sock' and she can count to two. She can say 'one, two.' " I had taught Gerri that myself yesterday and she'd picked it up fast. By next week I figured I'd have her counting to five.

Dad did not seem to be listening to me. "Look, Neil," he said, "Gerri will never get better. She'll never have any real sense."

It wasn't that Gerri didn't have any sense, it was just that she had her own kind of sense, but Dad didn't understand that.

A car had driven up behind ours and was honking, so Dad said I'd better get out and that he'd call me soon. I was sort of glad to leave because I didn't want to talk about Gerri any more. I wanted to get up to the apartment and tell my mother about the neat fish I'd caught. I'd tell Gerri too. If she didn't understand, I'd just show her a picture of a trout in the encyclopedia. Maybe I'd teach her to say "trout."

Dad rolled down the window to say good-by when I'd gotten out of the car, and all of a sudden, I thought of what he'd said about his moustache, how it was uncomfortable and got on his nerves, so he'd decided to get rid of it—*fffft*—and no kidding, it was like being hit with an icy wind when I realized that the way he felt about his moustache was exactly the way he felt about *us*.

"Remember, if you change your mind about moving in with me, call me any time, will you, Neil?" he said.

I said okay, but I didn't really think I'd change my mind. I didn't have any intention of moving out then, of leaving. I couldn't possibly guess that in a week's time, I'd be packing my own suitcase, saying good-by to my sister, and dialing my father's number to tell him to come and get me, fast.

nineteen

As soon as I walked in the door, my mother gave me the good news and the bad news about Gerri. The good news was that she'd slept through the night all night Saturday for the first time without banging her head. The bad news was that she'd wet her pants again, this time in public, at the zoo, when the elephant trumpeted and scared her out of her wits.

Other news was that Joe/Jason had called twice and wanted me to return his call as soon as I came home.

I was in no mood to dial Joe's number. "Aren't you going to call him?" my mother asked twice. "Too tired," I said. I didn't want to go into it about Joe. "Where's Gerri?" I asked. I wanted to tell them both about the fish.

"She's asleep. And you know what else, Neil?" my mother said. Her eyes opened really wide, like she was going to spring a biggie surprise. "When I was giving her a bath tonight after she messed herself up at the zoo, she started to sing the Battle Hymn of the Republic, can you believe that? She sang it all the way through. Well, she did put her own lyrics to it, but you know what, Neil? She never went off key, not once!"

"No kidding, Mom?"

"No kidding."

Joe/Jason came to my home room to see me first thing next morning. "Why didn't you return my call, Neil?" he said. "I have some colossal news."

"You won an Oscar." I tried to get my voice sounding real ex-friend cool. Who knows how many more people he'd educated about Geraldine and what colorful yarns he'd spun all over school about her?

"Please, baby, I told you it was a slip of the lip about your sister. Can't we bury it?"

"Okay, it's buried. Now what's the news?

"We all want you to play the Battle Hymn of the Republic in the Follies. All the kids who heard you Friday, that is. Everybody thinks you're great."

"What are you, putting me on? What happened, did Wendy break her fingers in a game or what?"

"She didn't break a thing, baby. She just thinks you'd be great doing that one number, that's all."

"What'd you do, pay her off or something?"

"Would I do that?" Joe/Jason said, and right

away his ears flamed up pink as rose petals. I couldn't even imagine what he'd promised Wendy to get her to give up that plum piece in the show. A sterling silver candelabra for her piano?

Or—aha!—I just remembered I'd heard she was flunking math. Joe/Jason was a star in math and knew all the algebra ropes, didn't he? "It's too late," I said. "The Follies is this Friday night, isn't it, Joe . . . er . . . Jason?"

"Listen, you've got it down pat already, so what's the problem?"

"How long did you promise to tutor Wendy?" I wanted to say, but I didn't. I didn't want his charity, no kidding, but all the same I did. I kept thinking how Dad would come to the Follies, and maybe sit in one of the front rows and applaud like crazy when I'd finished the piece, and how everyone in the school would see me up there too and stop overlooking me all the time. Most of all, I'd become part of the music/drama group and have somebody to sit in the cafeteria with and walk through the halls with and just plain hang around with. I wouldn't have to be a singles act anymore.

"Can I practice on the school piano? Our piano is —hmmm—out of tune," I said. No point in telling Joe/Jason *that* whole story.

"Sure, any time," Joe/Jason said, and he looked so relieved, I felt like I'd almost done him a favor.

I guess I never worked so hard in my life as I did that week. Although I knew the piece pretty well, knowing I was going to have to sit out there and play in front of two million people (well, a couple of hundred, anyway) gave me a headache that spread from my scalp right down to my knees.

Every day after school I'd sit working at it in the auditorium and still worry I might mess it up Friday night. Joe/Jason and the rest of the music/drama group were really in there for me, and everyone said I was putting real glory and hallelujah into it and it was going to be the highlight of the show.

By dress rehearsal I was pretty confident I'd do a fair job. I guess if I live to be two thousand I'll never forget how to play that piece, I'd played it so many times.

My number came just as Joe/Jason came downstage and announced he'd won the election and four girls danced out and threw red, white, and blue confetti all over him and sang "Congratulations, President Pierce!" "You'll stop the show!" a couple of the kids told me.

My mother had arranged for Mrs. Shrub to sit with Gerri so she could come to the performance, and of course I'd told Dad to come too. He sounded really pleased and said he'd pick Mom and me up Friday night and drive us to school very early to make sure he and Mom would get good seats up front.

My mother let down the sleeves of my old blue jacket that had gotten too small and sent it to the cleaners and bought me a new blue tie with little white musical notes on it, and left me a note in my room saying "Don't forget to shine your shoes!"

Gerri was still blamming her head against the wall, but now she skipped a night here and there, and her performances were down to about three or four blams per night. The night before the concert, I just lay awake waiting for her to start and that night she never did, but I hardly slept anyway.

I was jumpy all day Friday too and so was Joe/Jason—he said his mother was going to slip him one of her tranquilizers before show time—and the rest of the music/drama group was jittery too. Today for the first time, I sat with them in the cafeteria at lunch and even if I was no rajah, it was good to be in on everything and feel like part of a bunch.

My mother made my favorite casserole for dinner, but I hardly ate a bite. My eye was on the clock and so was my mother's. "Where is Mrs. Shrub?" she said a couple of times. "It's not like her to be late."

She hadn't arrived by the time my father came and buzzed from downstairs, signaling he was double-parked and wanted us to come down right away.

"I'll have to wait for Mrs. Shrub," my mother said, frowning. "You go ahead with Dad, and I'll follow in a taxi as soon as she gets here."

When I got downstairs and told my father, he

said he'd hold a place for my mother but we'd better hurry or the best seats would be gone. He said
he liked the way I looked and especially admired
my shined shoes. He thought they'd be wasted
under the piano and kiddingly suggested I plant
them right on top where everybody would see
them.

Everybody was in a frenzy of panic backstage.
Joe/Jason was practically green with fright under
his stage make-up because his mother had
changed her mind about the tranquilizer and had
given him milk with a shot of vanilla in it instead,
which he said made him even more nervous. The
only really cool performer was Wendy Wellington,
who had tied her hair some crazy new way on top
of her head, which made her look like her own
older sister and gave her the look of someone without a worry in the world.

I took a peek out at the overflow audience
through the side of the curtain and found my father, who had an aisle seat in the third row, but
the seat he was saving for my mother was still
empty. What if Mrs. Shrub didn't come? My
mother would never get to see me play!

But there was no time for worry; it was show
time!

The orchestra struck up, the curtain opened,
and Joe/Jason marched out on the stage to do his
opening number. He was great, he was terrific, he
was better than he'd ever been, and his first
number practically brought the house down. I

peeked out and saw my father applauding, looking as if he was really enjoying the show. The seat next to him was still empty.

Now Wendy Wellington stepped out and walked to the piano like performing was something she did twice a week, and played, "Congratulations, Mrs. Pierce," and I did hear her make one or two little mistakes but I think the audience missed them, because she also got a great bunch of applause when she was finished.

By this time I was a trembling wreck knowing I'd be on right after the next number, and starting to feel cramps that jumped from one part of my body to another. One minute I'd get this tight feeling in my neck and the next minute it jumped down into my wrist, then it landed in my fingers.

"Neil, you're on!"

I walked out of the side stage door to the piano, and right away Rich Whitefield, the kid in charge of lighting, turned the pink spotlight on me. My legs felt like a couple of paper drinking straws that might fold right up under me in any old direction. I don't really know how I made it, but here I was, sitting on the piano bench in the middle of the pink spotlight, the whole place quieter than the public library, everybody in the audience waiting for me to begin. I was to start playing and the action would begin onstage after I'd played eight bars, but now I felt as if ten million eyes were on me, ten million ears were tuned in my direction, ready for me to hit the first note. The auditorium was dark, so I couldn't tell if my mother had arrived, but it was too late to worry about that now.

I began to play, concentrating with every spark plug in my head, letting my fingers remember each plink and plunk, getting the horsepower into my hands, and, like Dad had told me, going easy on the right pedal. I relaxed . . . it was working! My fingers took over and zipped along like they belonged to someone else, maybe Tchaikovsky. The keyboard felt like velvet and the tempo was perfect. The cramps disappeared; I was really proud of myself.

Then!

I heard a laugh from the back of the auditorium: *Ha, hee, hi, ho yeeeeee!*

NO!

It was like someone shot me right in the stomach with an icicle.

YeeeeeeEEEEEEEEEEEEEE!

The spark plugs exploded in my head, the horsepower went dead in my hands, and the plinks and the plunks turned into blangs and blongs. Gerri was somewhere out there (had my mother lost her mind, bringing her here?), and although it was dark and I couldn't see, I went cold as a corpse thinking she was headed this way—was going to try to—oh, good, grey grief—climb on this piano?

Sure enough, the sound came closer. *YeeeEEEEE!*

My fingers died on the keys. The audience stirred. Someone laughed.

I heard my mother's voice, whisper-calling "Geraldine! Come back here!"

More laughter. Feet scraped. People began buzzing. I heard Joe/Jason's voice snapping at me from behind the curtain. "Play, Neil, play!"

I couldn't play. I could hardly breathe.

"Geraldine!" cried my mother's anxious voice. Shuffle/shuffle footsteps came nearer.

Now I could see her dim form shuffle/shuffling right towards me. No hand from heaven was coming down to grab me, nobody was going to save me from this here-and-now, real-live nightmare.

"Play, Neil, for pity's sake, play!" Joe/Jason sounded pretty hysterical, but my fingers were finished and useless, like a steam-roller had just gone over them.

The audience was now out-and-out laughing, snickering, scraping their feet, even clapping.

Geraldine was practically at the piano. I saw my mother weaving through the standees in the aisle, trying to get at her to grab her.

I heard her say, "Come back, Geraldine!" and then—rock bottom—Gerri yelled, like an echo in the mountains, "Gelldeen. Gellydeen GELLY-DEEN!" and it didn't take more than two seconds for three or four East-Enders in the first two rows to pick it up and yell, "Jellybean! Hey, Jellybean!" and pretty soon somebody from the back joined in and then it was all you could hear, *Jellybean, Jellybean, HEY, JELLYBEAN!* until the whole auditorium was in pandemonium.

That was it. My mother grabbed Gerri just as she reached the piano, and Mr. Peck got up to restore order, but it was all over for me.

My hands were shaking like ashes in a wind, and Wendy Wellington had to come to the piano to finish the Battle Hymn of the Republic. The show must go on and the show did go on, but it went on without me. My sister had finally learned to say her own name, sort of, but at that point even if she'd recited the Declaration of Independence I wouldn't have cared.

I hardly remember how I got out of the school and into the car. My father drove us all home, and no one said a word except my mother, who explained that Mrs. Shrub's back went bad on the way over to our house and she called from a phone booth to say she was sorry she couldn't come but she was going home in a taxi to lie on a board. My mother aplogized five times for bringing Gerri, but said she just couldn't miss the show. She said she'd warned Gerri about behaving and that she'd stayed way back and held Gerri's hand but that when Gerri saw me she went wild and tore away from her and practically whizzed down the aisle, squeezing between people who were standing there and squiggling through to where my mother couldn't reach her. My mother said she'd never forgive herself, *never*, and then she was quiet too, just looking out of the window of the car as if she was letting the quiet and the dark sift right into her skin and bones.

That night, Gerri's head-banging was worse than it had been in weeks. While I was lying there listening to the thumps, I realized Dad had been right all along: I'd be better off living with him, and the sooner I moved out of here, the better. I couldn't face going back to school Monday anyway. Or ever. I'd call Dad first thing in the morning to tell him to come and get me as soon as possible. Right away. *Now*.

twenty

I never did get to sleep that night. I just lay awake until it got light, watching my room go from black to blue-black to misty-grey, thinking and thinking, waiting for it to get late enough to call Dad. Just as he said, there was no use trying to stay here with Mom and Gerri. Who could predict what more crazy things Gerri might do to wreck my life? She hadn't stopped the head-banging, so Mr. Parrish would probably be back again with another petition (maybe even the police next time) and the neighbors would keep right on hating us, people would go right on staring at her in the streets wherever we went, kids would probably go on throwing pebbles, maybe even rocks, at her when they saw her in the park, the way they did the one time I took her, and other mothers would keep their children as far away from Gerri as they could in the playground, as always.

If I moved in with Dad, it might even be easier for Mom. One kid is easier to take care of than two, and Mom could give Gerri my room and turn Gerri's room back into a dining room.

At five sharp, I slipped out of bed, got dressed, and went down to the storage room to get my old suitcase. It was dark and spooky down there and for a minute I was tempted to wait until it brightened up, later, but my mind was made up. I didn't want to waste time. Without waking a soul, I brought the suitcase up in the elevator, let myself back into our apartment, and went to my room to get ready.

As early as it was, I wasn't alone long. How could Gerri have heard me creeping around like a mouse in my room? I'll never know. All I know is that she suddenly appeared in my doorway, the wool scarfs still tied around her head, with that clean-slate expression on her face that looked as if she was still in the middle of a dream.

"Go back to sleep, Gerri," I whispered. I didn't want to wake Mom, not now.

Gerri just stood there, mouth open, head to one side, watching me open drawers, take out socks, shirts, and underwear, reminding me of the way she'd watched Dad when he was packing to leave.

"Go back to bed, willya?" I whispered again, but she wasn't leaving. Her eyes were just following me and watching every move like she couldn't believe what she was seeing.

"Willya stop staring at me, for pity's sake?" I said, and Gerri said, "Blixen, vixen, Gellybeen," and a little saliva stayed in the corner of her mouth.

I thought if I ignored her, she'd pretty soon get bored watching me and go back to bed, but no luck. She took a step into my room and then another step and then—believe it or not—she started to *un*pack my open suitcase, take out the socks, the shirts, the underwear, and try to stuff them back into all the wrong drawers!

"Cut it out, Geraldine!" I hissed at her, "Just stop it!" but she wouldn't listen. Out came all the stuff I'd put in, the shirts, the belt, two of my photo albums, and the camera, and all the time she was shuffling around undoing all my work, her nose was getting redder and redder like she'd been out in a snowstorm and was catching a terrible cold and was going to sneeze up the place in about a minute and a half.

It made me good and mad that she wouldn't listen, although I'd told her to get out and leave my things alone about ten times, so I grabbed her by the shoulders and stuffed her into a chair and looked at her with real murder in my eye and ordered her not to dare get up or I'd have to get real tough.

That did it. She just sat there, not daring to move, watching everything I did, too scared to say a word and looking as if I'd already punched her in the nose.

I repacked the suitcase, and closed it. Half my stuff was still lying around my room, but I guessed Dad would come and pick it up for me later. For now, I had enough to see me through a couple of weeks. I was set to go.

I heard my mother stir in her room, heard the bedsprings creak, and held my breath. Had all the commotion waked her? But no, she'd probably just turned over in bed; being up half the night with Gerri usually meant she'd sleep late, especially Saturday mornings.

It was almost six, still probably too early to call Dad, but I'd try anyway. If he knew I wanted to come live with him, he'd pick me up right away, I was sure.

I closed the kitchen door and dialed Dad's number. He didn't answer for the longest time; ten rings, then eleven. What if he wasn't home?

"Hullo?"

Of course, he'd been fast asleep, and his voice sounded like it was coming through a tunnel from the center of the earth.

I told him to come and get me, but I had to tell him three times before he understood. Finally he caught on. His voice got a bounce in it. "I'll be right there," he said, and he told me to meet him out front with my suitcase. Then he said, "I'll hurry, Neil. I'll be right there," and he hung up.

I went back to my room. Gerri was still sitting in there where I'd left her, slumped in the same chair, looking like a bunch of old clothes somebody had left in a pile to go to the laundry, staring at my suitcase like any minute snakes were going to pop out of it.

"Cheer up, Gerri," I said. I went over and took the wool scarfs off her head. "I'll visit often, no kidding."

Gerri didn't answer.

I went to my desk and wrote a note to Mom and stuck it on my dresser, where she couldn't miss it and Gerri couldn't reach it. After what happened last night, Mom would understand.

Then I picked up my suitcase and tiptoed out of my room.

I crossed the living room and walked to the foyer practically holding my breath.

I heard a sound and spun around. Gerri had followed me. She was standing right where the piano had been, in the empty corner, not daring to get closer.

"Go back to bed," I whispered.

Gerri's mouth opened wide, it closed, it opened. Then Gerri said, "Neil."

Or was I hearing things?

"Neil." She said it again, clear as anything. "Neil." She'd learned to say my name. "Neil, Neil." No kidding.

Well, so what?

Learning a simple name like Neil was no big deal.

"Good-by, Gerri. Thanks for learning my name, but I'm leaving," I said.

I walked out of the apartment, got in the elevator, and relaxed. I would not be meeting Mr. Rasmussen at this hour of the morning; none of the other petition-signers was likely to be on the elevator either, giving me the evil eye or making remarks. The floors slid by—five—four—three—two. At each floor, I could swear I heard Gerri saying it again, as if her voice were following me all the way from upstairs: *Neil, Neil, Neil.*

The elevator stopped, the door slid open.

I picked up my suitcase and walked across the lobby, through the glass doors, and outside, onto the sidewalk. It must have rained during the night, because the sidewalk was damp around the cracks and there was a puddle in the gutter. The air smelled like laundry soap and the sky wasn't blue yet, but it looked like it was trying.

I saw the ord coming down the street, slowing down. It pulled to the curb right in front of me. My father, without his moustache, smiled at me.

"Do you need a hand with the suitcase, Neil?" he asked.

Suddenly I could hardly see my father, the damp sidewalk, the sky, or anything; everything blurred up like somebody had turned a sprinkler on behind my eyes. I blinked and my father said, "What's wrong, Neil?" or something like that. I'm not sure what he said because there was interference; it was ricocheting from the sky or my head or from over the rainbow, for all I knew; it was Gerri's voice saying, "Neil," and no kidding, it was putting a firecracker right in my heart.

"Neil, what's the matter?" my father asked.

I couldn't say it; it just jammed up in my throat like old rags, that not everybody can have perfect pitch, that even though Gerri would always be strange/different/funny/weird, she was the way she was, and she was my sister.

The music/drama kids would tear me to shreds because of her Monday, but they're regular kids, so sooner or later even Joe/Jason might forgive me.

Dad curled his fingers around the steering wheel, then he uncurled them. "You've changed your mind, haven't you, Neil?" he said.

I nodded. I wished like anything he hadn't shaved his moustache. Maybe he'd give it another chance, sometime.

"I understand," he said, looking straight out the windshield so he wouldn't have to see me standing there sniffing and looking stupid and not knowing what to say. "Maybe one day I'll change mine," he said.

"You mean you'll come home?"

My father didn't answer for what seemed like a long time. Then he said, "Not now, not right now," and he cleared his throat. "I'll call you soon, Neil," he said, and I picked up my suitcase and watched him pull away from the curb. I stood a while, thinking about it. "Not right now" didn't mean "never," did it?

I turned, went back inside, and pushed the elevator button. Almost immediately the elevator door opened and Mr. Rasmussen stepped out with his Scottie dog on a leash. At this hour!

"Good morning, Mr. Rasmussen," I said, quaking as usual at the very sight of him.

"Good morning," Mr. Rasmussen said, almost cordially, and as he stepped aside, he held the door so it wouldn't slide closed on my suitcase as I was lifting it into the elevator.

"Thank you," I said, but Mr. Rasmussen kept holding the door, as if he was waiting to tell me something but didn't know how to say it. Finally he said, "Your sister is really coming along, isn't she?"

I was so surprised I guess I just stood there, half in the elevator and half out of it.

"She brought some scraps to my dog the other day and I really appreciate it."

"She did?"

"It was very thoughtful, and he loved every last bite. Except—" Mr. Rasmussen then smiled. *Smiled.* Showed his teeth, at least ten of them. I couldn't believe it. "Except the marshmallows. I'm afraid he's not much for marshmallows," he said.

My sister, now smart enough to push the right elevator buttons, to say my name so anybody could understand it, to bring leftovers to a dog—and getting smarter by the minute. *Really coming along.* Even Mr. Rasmussen had noticed it.

My own voice came out of nowhere. "She's getting there," I said, proud as anything. She's all right, no kidding, I thought as the door of the elevator slid closed and the elevator began moving up.